the impossible blonde

or my name is Sally

a Nathalie Endeavour story

I'd like to say that I fell in love with Sally Twitchett the first time I met her. It appeals to my sense of the romantic and she is so spectacular it should have been true. However, it wouldn't be an accurate description of what happened. It is true that the first time I met her I was absolutely stunned and was desperate to be close to her. From those first moments I was infatuated and within days did fall hopelessly in love with her; but Sally is a difficult and complex girl and fabulous as she is I wasn't ever sure how to deal with her.

I suppose it would be best to start from the beginning. Meeting Sally was the start of something wonderful that would also eventually break my heart, but it was also part of a scary time I would nonetheless gladly relive a thousand times just to experience again those wonderful months with her.

Let me start with who I am. I like to think of myself as a bit of an adventurer. What this really means is that I hate the idea of doing anything approximating what most would call a *proper job*. I'm not completely unreliable or lazy, but unless I have to, I don't work. One of the reasons for that is that I get bored incredibly quickly; bored with situations, jobs, scenery and people. Even women. This means I seek out opportunities that allow me to make money and have some fun at the same time. Throw in some thrills and adventure and I'm a very happy boy. But even this isn't enough to keep me at something for long. Don't get me wrong – if I take on a job I finish it. If I don't think I can go the distance, I don't start. Before you start thinking of me as some kind of action hero let me be clear: the sort of jobs I take on don't usually involve any heroics and they aren't usually glamorous. Once in a while I get to stay in a flashy hotel, put my foot down in a hired car and even come across the occasional beautiful girl - but overall they're mostly pretty dull jobs although not what most men would think of as normal everyday work. Sometimes (but rarely) I get to do someone a good deed.

When asked and if I want to be honest I describe myself as a *Sort of part time private eye* and this usually causes eyebrows to rise and interest to be piqued in men and women alike. It doesn't really describe me at all. What I do is loaf around until I run out of money then try to ingratiate myself with someone stupid enough to pay me to do something I convince them needs doing. These people are always well off enough (I don't take from those who can't afford it) not to worry when they realise I wasn't really necessary. Here's a recent example of an opportunity that demonstrates the low level to which I will sink when desperate:

I was drinking in a bar with my last twenty quid, mixing it up with a couple of drunk, middle-aged men with more money than they know what to do with. One was American. He and his wife were in Paris (I'd fetched up there broke and had to work in an English-owned restaurant for four weeks to get a stake to release me to the higher life) for a month. Wife wanted nothing to do with him, he moaned after too many glasses of Cutty Sark, and he'd hardly seen her since they arrived. He suspected she found shopping more interesting than their marriage. I subtly suggested this was a curious matter perhaps worthy of looking into. After half an hour he was convinced she was having a ffair and told me everything he knew about his English wife's previous irtation with French life. Another twenty minutes and three more double vhiskies later he hired me, although he made it seem as if I was doing him an normous favour (or maybe I convinced him that I was) by agreeing to follow er and find out what she was up to.

did follow her and I did find out exactly what she was up to.

/hen Marina Jones (the wife's real name) was seventeen she travelled to aris with an older female friend. They had enjoyed a wonderful trip and larina had fallen in love with a Parisian waiter. A short time after she turned home she found she was pregnant. Marina's father, influenced by s wife and the love he had for his only daughter, agreed that she could turn to Paris to see the man she claimed was the love of her life and the iild's father. As it turned out, he wasn't a complete bastard and promised to ve and cherish Marina if only she could be permitted to remain. She turned ghteen before the baby was born and her parents agreed to her staying in rance. The mother flew back and forth regularly to see all was well.

ie sad ending to Marina's story was that her French bloke set up his own staurant which became very successful. Marina seriously got into spending s money while the child was looked after by a succession of nannies. One ay Marina fell in love with another man. She was still young, drank too much id had come to the conclusion that motherhood was not her thing. At least it until the boy grew older and became interesting. So she left her son with s father and went off to enjoy the high life with some Greek who owned any ships and had many millions to play with.

ears went by, Marina always intending to go back and see her son but never iite managing to get away from the possessively charming and utterly ntrolling Greek. She left him when she realised she was a complete isoner, but by the time she returned to Paris her son was gone. His father d sold the restaurant and nobody knew where they were. Heartbroken, arina vowed to lead a better life, to be a decent woman and to never give up the search for her son.

ore years went by and Marina hit thirty. She had given up on her son and in general. Her parents died, her father of cancer and her mother in a car ash. She had no other family. She left England in desperation and had und work as a secretary in New York.

arina married her boss, the man I convinced to hire me to investigate her spected infidelity. Only Marina had not been unfaithful. She had given her sband a son and a daughter and had been the best wife she knew how to . One day she had received word from her son, now a young adult, that he s alive and his father dead. Marina had come to Paris to meet him, having nvinced her husband that the children could be left with their American aunt d uncle for a month of fun.

Before you start thinking badly about me, let me reassure you that Marina's husband never learnt the truth. She was utterly convinced that if he found out about what she considered her dreadful past, he would be heartbroken. He was not, she told me, an experienced man and held very *"old fashioned"* views on life. He was a devoted husband and father and she trusted him without question but could never let him know the truth about her past.

I told Marina's husband she was just enchanted again by Paris and was re-visiting her youth and shopping. There was absolutely nothing to worry about. I even gave him back half of the outrageous fee I'd charged him.

So you see, I do have principles. Which Sally noted quickly as we got to know each other. Nothing gets past Sally, you see, despite her sometimes vacant and often inappropriate presentation. And despite what you may come to think of the beautiful blonde with the super-model looks and the often bored or frivolous attitude, Sally Twitchett is the most principled, decent woman I have ever met, as well as the most beautiful, maddening and sad.

*   *   *   *   *

The chap called Timothy Maitland (not his real name, of course) had crossed my path several times in the first five days of my current job. Coincidence, I assumed, because Gstaad is not a huge place and if you were moving in the circles I was, you frequented a small number of places often.

The job: I had been hired to track down (well, *follow* because his whereabouts were already known) a man who had stolen another man's wife and a lot of valuable jewellery and bonds along with her. My mission was simple: pin them down, get into their suite at the Palace (the only hotel to stay in Gstaad if you are anybody and have money) and steal back the jewellery and bonds. My employer wasn't bothered about his wife. He would soon get another. I had exercised my moral discretion by enquiring why the police could not be involved but, of course, the jewellery was his wife's and as for the bonds … well, there would be complications …

Sure. So I took the job because I was broke. In fact, I sought it out through an acquaintance of an acquaintance.

I'd found the couple, engaged the guy in conversation – he seemed like a reasonable chap – and learnt of their hopes. She was beautiful and having met my employer, I could understand why she would prefer this bloke. Only he was a thief. It was obvious. So I wasn't bothered about stealing from them what they had stolen, and ruining their hopes of living in happiness and enjoying the high life.

Maitland, I discovered, was also watching the couple. He clocked me immediately, of course, and obviously knew I was watching them and planning something. But he never said a word. He engaged me in conversation about all sorts of interesting stuff and he knew that I knew we were both thinking the same things and watching each other carefully.

When the girl with the chestnut hair arrived, I couldn't believe my eyes. Maitland seemed to have a relationship with this stunning beauty that wasn't the usual thing. They were pretending, I could tell. She was dazzling. Tall, gorgeous, a bit athletic, a tennis player almost certainly and she had the biggest, round emerald green eyes I have ever seen. She seemed totally in control and when she spoke it was with confidence and an attitude that said *don't mess with me.* She walked past me once, deliberately I know and I was impressed. The silk dress – Dior I reckoned – was a killer, just short enough but not as daring as many these days and she was perfect. I couldn't help turning and watching the girl I learnt was called Nathalie as she walked out. Every man there did.

Maitland sat beside me and sighed. 'I know. You don't need to tell me.'

'She's …'

'As I said: you don't need to tell me.'

'Is she your …?' I left it unfinished.

'Yes and no. When it suits her. When it doesn't …' He lifted his Martini, sipped, made a flippant gesture with his right hand and the gold Rolex sparkled.

'What does she do?' I asked, when I really meant *"What are you two up to?"*

'She owns a very successful boutique. King's Road, London.'

'Oh.' I know the King's Road well. 'What's it called?'

'Uzz.'

'Very trendy.'

'Yes. It is. Very successful. She's loaded.'

'Why the long face?'

'Have I? How long are you around for?'

'I hope at least three score years and ten.'

'I meant in Gstaad.'

'Now you did. Until I finish what I came here for.' No point in playing games.

'Look.' Maitland put down his glass, stood, leaned on the walnut bar and looked at me with a serious expression. 'I don't know for certain what you're here for. But I have an idea. Take some advice: finish up quickly and get out.'

I knew someone had seen me earlier, when I slipped the stolen key into the door of the hotel suite.

'I wish I knew what the hell you're talking about' I said flippantly. 'Another G & T?'

'No, I'll have a vodka Martini.' Maitland looked at the barman. 'And I couldn't give a damn how you make it. I'm not like that twit in the books.'

'I beg your pardon sir?' The barman was genuinely puzzled, but I'd got it.

'He means shaken or stirred' I offered. 'James Bond always insists on it being shaken.'

'Ah, 007!' The young barman grinned. 'Shaken not stirred, yes?'

'Stirred, shaken, anyway you like so long as it's not done in the glass. It's not how you mix it - it's the proportions.' Maitland gave the barman instructions and added 'And make sure you drizzle a little vermouth around the glass before you fill it. And just a sliver of lemon peel on the rim.'

'So what brings you and Nathalie to the land of clocks and cheese?' I didn't expect an answer.

Maitland shook his Rolex. 'I want another, from the source, not some twit in Bond Street. But we're thinking of investing in property here.'

'Really?' I arched an eyebrow so as to say *"Pull the other one, it's got sleigh bells on it."* The way he looked at me made me feel an idiot and way out of m depth.

We drank and made small talk. I didn't feel confident about probing any more There was something about him. He didn't ring true and I saw bad things in his eyes. I was beginning to wish I'd never met him.

After another five minutes Maitland was joined by a big English bloke. Immaculately dressed in a roll neck sweater, black slacks and a blue blazer with enough shiny buttons to dazzle an Admiral, he must have been well ove six feet tall and looked very fit and very strong. He eyed me professionally, dismissed me as any kind of threat and slapped Maitland on the back as he said 'Found you at last!'

'I'm not that hard to find' Maitland said. 'Oh, by the by, this is ...' He turned t me and raised his eyebrows.

No one of interest' I said, downing my glass and standing. 'I'll see you round.'

I had a very bad feeling about the two of them. They were clearly not what they seemed and were up to something I knew I didn't want to know about.

I'd got the bonds and some of the jewellery. They'd been pretty well hidden but I'm good at finding hidden things. I hadn't seen the couple or heard anything from anyone that suggested they were on to me or had even noticed the stuff had gone. They'd been daily regulars in the bars and restaurants we frequented but there hadn't been any sign of them for more than two days.

I must admit, I was feeling troubled. I was, after all, no more than a common thief. I don't know what had made me stick around but I suddenly realised it was time to get out. And there had been Maitland's obvious warning.

*   *   *   *   *

I didn't see it coming. The evening was chill, but as usual in this part of the world, not unpleasantly so. There was a light dusting of snow, but it was firm underfoot. As I walked to the hired Mercedes after one too many glasses of brandy, I went down. I thought that I'd slipped, but when I saw the girl's face, contorted with anger and rage, and the ski pole in her hands, I knew that whoever was behind me had pushed me. A second later I saw his face, calm but focussed on stopping the girl bringing the ski pole down on me while he pulled the Mauser or whatever weird handgun it was from his jacket.

Then two things happened at once. I was still on the ground when I saw Maitland grab the bloke and wrench the gun from his hand. The woman called Nathalie walked brusquely up to the girl with the ski pole and punched her in the face. She went down like the proverbial sack of spuds and Nathalie didn't even stop in her stride. She frowned at me as she walked off into the snow and the lights towards the hotel.

Maitland had put the bloke down in a second and he regarded me with a puzzled expression.

'You're not cut out for this, old man' Maitland said calmly and held out a hand.

As I pulled myself up I noticed Nathalie had stopped under a light and was talking with two people. It looked like the big man I'd seen briefly in the bar and there was another girl, tall, dark haired. They spoke for a minute and then went their separate ways. I couldn't catch their words, but I could hear their voices and the girl's voice was definitely foreign, Eastern by the sound of it.

There was obviously much more to Maitland than I had figured.

'Thanks' was all I could manage to say.

Maitland didn't reply. He was rifling through the girl's pockets and then the bloke's. When he stood up he regarded both of them as if he couldn't make up his mind.

'What do you want me to do with them?' he asked after a moment.

'What?'

'Well, they're part of your bloody mess. Do you want them left here or do yo want to dispose of them?'

'Dispose …?'

'You really are playing out of your league, aren't you? Look; if we leave ther here, they won't involve the Police; but they will come looking for you again. I'm surprised you didn't spot them when you left the bar - they couldn't have been more conspicuous.'

I felt even worse.

'She got you with the ski stick. You're bleeding.'

I put a hand to my face where something was beginning to ache. There wa blood on it.

Maitland took me into the bar, straight into the Gent's, helped me clean up and then bought me two large brandies straight off, even 'though I'd alread had too many. The incident had sobered me up a bit.

'Look, it's not what you think you know.'

I looked at him as if he was barmy.

'You needn't look so surprised!' He grinned. He looked like a bloody film st a bit too flash, gleaming white teeth, immaculate blonde hair in an up to the minute style and his clothes were very smooth.

'Look, I don't know who you people are, but …'

'People?' Maitland drank and smiled again.

'Well; you're obviously some sort of team …'

'We're old friends on a trip that includes business as well as pleasure. Don go jumping to conclusions old man.'

He sounded like James bloody Bond.

More importantly … your round by the way … who exactly are you and what are you up to?'

Before I could answer the big man appeared to my rear right.

'Funny you should ask that, old chap' said Big Bloke to Maitland. 'The boss wants to know who this clown is. Not my words, by the way, old son.'

They saw me to a table in a corner, well out of earshot of everybody else and in the most polite and pleasant way pumped me for information. I was in no fit state to resist. And why should I? These people – Maitland particularly – had literally saved my life. If it hadn't been for him I would have been shot, stabbed, beaten. Yes, Nathalie floored the woman who would have opened my head with the stick, but nonetheless …

The big bloke introduced himself as Harry Halmer. I think it was a play on Harry from the Harry Palmer films based on the books by Len Deighton – you know, *Funeral in Berlin, Ipcress File, Horse Under Water* etc (don't think they've made that into a film yet); although of course in the books the spy geezer is anonymous. Anyway, he seemed quite affable and after a few drinks it was obvious he and Maitland were old colleagues.

'Well' HH said – he said that was what people called him – 'you've got yourself into a bit of a mess, old son. Those people you thought were merely doing the dirty on your boss are dirtier than you thought. They're mixed up with someone of interest to Her Majesty's Government …'

'You mean you.' I thought I might as well come out with it.

'Us?' HH laughed. 'Blimey, you reckon we work for the Government? That's a laugh. Security, mate. I was in the Navy, true …'

'Royal Marines' Maitland added as if I should be impressed 'but only a sergeant.'

'What about your boss?'

'Our who?' HH looked at Maitland, who'd said call him TM.

'Nathalie' I offered.

This time it was Maitland who laughed. 'Her? S'truth!'

He sat back and regarded me as if I was a simple schoolboy. 'Stop drawing conclusions. You've got it all wrong. Nathalie is a distraction. His, largely.' He nodded at TM. 'She fancies herself as a bit of a liberated bird and never misses the opportunity to make a man feel useless. That's why she enjoyed the opportunity of making you look pathetic by decking the girl with the ski stick.'

'Thanks.' My glass was empty.

'My boss' HH began as if he had decided to confide in me 'is a high-roller who employs me to sort out his security when he travels. He –' he jabbed a finger at TM – 'is an old school chum that I throw a few jobs to now and then. Now, my boss is a very well connected chap and he'd heard about your two lovebirds doing the dirty on one of his club members. Beginning to see the connections?'

'I think so …' I was, but I was also very suspicious and didn't believe most of it.

'He was worried they were in Gstaad because he was.'

'But who is he?'

'Sssshhh!' HH was obviously enjoying the secrecy. 'We mustn't use his name now, must we? Anyway … we two are watching them and we spot you watching them too. Then our boss tells us that one of his connections has found out your targets are in league with the Russians and the Secret Service are interested in them.'

'Russians …!?'

'Keep your voice down, old man.' TM regarded me with patient annoyance. He looked as if he were getting fed up with HH and his story, which made me even more suspicious.

'Yes. *Russkies*. Which makes it all the more difficult for you, I'm afraid.'

HH sat back and fiddled with his empty glass.

'So. What do I do now, then?'

'Well' HH sat forward again 'you can't go to the police. After all, you stole from them, did you not? And you said the jewellery was the girl's. Even if she is a Commie, they're her property.'

'True. Well, the Government then …'

'What are you going to say? Sorry, but I just blundered into some business with these two people who are hooked up with the Russians, who by the way I've stolen from and apparently your Secret Service people are interested in them and I might have cocked it up. Wouldn't go down very well, would it?'

'Then what the hell do I do? I'll leave. Tomorrow.'

No.' TM was firm. 'I don't think that's a good idea. You'd be followed. Then, when the time was right …'

You think they'd kill me?'

Don't you think they intended to do that tonight? They're a vicious lot, these Commie bastards.' TM sounded as if he was enjoying himself.

Oh God …' I must have sounded quite pathetic.

Look.' HH was conspiratorial. 'We're well set up here. We're pretty much up to anything and my boss can speak with the … well, let's say official people if they make an appearance. Your two will either be on the run now or will move on pretty damned quickly. When they discover you're with us, they'll probably back off. They've got limited time now. If they stick around too long trying to nobble you they'll get picked up by Her Majesty's whoever.' He sat back and smiled. 'In the meantime, you can hang out with us and we will afford you, for the minimal fee of plenty of good booze, our protection. How does that sound?'

don't believe you.' I thought I'd show some guts but I was still worried as well. 'The whole thing sounds bloody fishy to me. Sorry. Thanks for the help but I can't believe what you're saying.'

Hold on. Just give it a bit of thought, old man.' HH was on his feet and getting his wallet out. 'I'll get us some more drinks, then I need to make a quick phone call.' He ordered drinks and I saw him talking quietly into a telephone for about a minute.

Fifteen minutes later I was even worse for drink and the booze kept coming. I have to admit I was scared and didn't know what the hell to do. I was scared to leave the bar and of the two men. I owed my life to one of them, true, but he was clearly not happy to let me leave. I wouldn't take on either of them but was also scared to stay with them because I didn't believe a word they were saying.

Then she arrived. Not Sally. That would come soon enough. Tall, in a leather coat with a fur collar, boots, long gypsy-style dress and a fur hat and she had the most incredible inky black hair I've ever seen. It flowed over her shoulders and hung down over the left side of her face. She sat at the bar and a man I had never seen before walked to her and they exchanged a few words. They drank for a few minutes and then I heard her speaking in a language I identified straight away, although I don't speak a word of Russian.

s that …?'

Looks like it old man' TM said, shifting his chair so that he and HH were obscuring the Russian's view of me. 'Perhaps you might want to rethink your reaction to our offer.'

'Bloody hell!' I downed the rest of the brandy and almost choked. 'Bloody hell!'

'Calm old man, calm. No need for panic. She's leaving and she obviously wasn't here for you.' TM tried to look at me sympathetically, but his eyes were cold.

'But they *are* here. The Russians!'

'Who can tell?' The big man spread his hands. He smiled at TM and winked. He actually winked as he said 'Mysterious lot these Russian women, eh old chap?'

*   *   *   *   *

So they moved me from the hotel to the lodge where they were staying. I protested, but they put it politely, saying they couldn't risk my wandering around in case the Russians came for me. They also didn't know what they'd be called on to do and they didn't want me causing problems for them. What they meant was they wanted to keep me under constant watch for their own reasons.

The next afternoon Nathalie came and practically ignored me. She talked small talk and ski clothes to TM, who seemed very bored. She took two phone calls, which I thought odd as she was staying elsewhere, and then left.

For the next forty eight hours either HH or TM would leave the lodge at various times including through the night. They didn't know I clocked them doing it. Sometimes they didn't return until almost dawn. I didn't dare ask them what they were up to. I figured they weren't going to kill me or they would have done it already. They had every chance. But I was very definitely under their house arrest.

I had convinced myself I craved action and adventure. Well, now I bloody well had it in spades. I would be lucky to get out alive. I focussed on that; it made being cooped up more bearable.

I was in the lodge for three days. I rambled on a fair bit about myself, encouraged by them and the booze they kept dishing out as if it were water and was surprised at how tough I made myself sound. Then, one day, TM told me with a smile on his face that everything was all right. My lovebirds, as he referred to them, had left Gstaad and there were no Russians on the scene. I was a free man. I could go.

The problem was I had nowhere *to* go. I was broke. Sure, I had the jewellery which had been reported stolen so I couldn't safely get rid of it and I had the bonds, which were also hot. And without further contact with my employer who turned out to be mixed up with all kinds of dodgy doings, I had no fee. Down and out in Gstaad! What a joke.

was interesting how quickly the threat of losing my life ceased to be my reoccupation and not having any viable options for the immediate future consumed my thoughts.

The problem didn't task me for long, however. I'd pretty much made up my mind to cross over into France and TM insisted I borrow some money from him. I asked how I could return it and he told me I could send a cheque for him care of the Fuzz boutique in the King's Road Chelsea. I doubted whether the place even existed but had agreed, when I thought I was going to die for the second time in seventy two hours.

There were noises from outside and then the door burst open.

It was her - the Russian woman. Only this time she wasn't wearing a coat; just a long black gypsy-style skirt and a plain black silk blouse. She looked fierce but devastatingly beautiful. The Luger in her hand was aimed straight at the centre of my forehead and she just stood there in the door, breathing heavily.

I didn't look at TM or HH and I couldn't move my arms to raise them. I actually closed my eyes and when the bang came I jumped out of my skin. But I didn't die.

The bang was the beauty I learnt was Alexandra Krosova slamming the door.

'Are you G and T today or vodka?' HH's voice came from my left and I looked he raised eyebrows at the Russian and grinned. She scowled at me and strode past.

' of no difference. And trouble is gone.' As she walked past me I got a scent that was intoxicating and unusual, like cinnamon and honey with a touch of lemon. Her voice was low, strong, but feminine. As I relaxed and accepted she wasn't the enemy I quickly found her fascinating, although she still scares the hell out of me.

Alexandra sat in a chair close to TM who seemed totally unbothered and was actually looking through a magazine. She drank the gin and tonic HH had given her and regarded me as if I were an annoying cat, or dog. When she had finished her drink she merely held out the empty glass and HH took and filled it.

'Why he is still here?' she asked TM.

'Safest place for him. We'd just about thought the coast was clear and were going to dispatch him to the French border.' TM looked at me with what I thought might have been sympathy before he carried on. 'Now I suppose we'll have to nurse maid him until we can think of what to do with him next. Unless the boss is just going to cast him adrift and let him take his chances. Sorry old man, but you might have to face up to that.'

I didn't know what to say when Alexandra said 'Opezdol!'

'I beg your pardon?' I looked at her and was mesmerised, the way you sometimes do with something that's going to do you great harm. She looked very angry.

'She said you're an idiot. That's right isn't it Alexandra?' HH seemed pleased with himself when she nodded curtly.

'If you're in league with the Russians …' I started to put it together and felt very threatened.

'Well, only so much as she's Russian and on the team.' TM put down the magazine and stood up, crossed to the drinks trolley, poured a very large whisky and soda and handed it to me.

'I knew you were a lying pair!'

Alexandra sighed with dramatic effect, stood so quickly that I jumped visibly again and poured herself vodka. When neither of the blokes said anything sh shouted 'For sake of God! Tell him! He knows much already so tell him!'

'You were right' HH said in an almost apologetic tone. 'We are working on something for the Government.'

'Then you *are* Secret Service …'

'No' HH said emphatically. '*I'm* not.'

I looked at TM, who held up his hands palms outward 'And I'm not either. We just … help out when our boss needs us to.' He looked at Alexandra. 'But *sh* is.'

I looked at Alexandra who seemed a little more relaxed. She shook her head and muttered 'Stupid little boy' and got more vodka.

'She's …' I looked from TM to HH to Alexandra and back again. She leaned against the drinks cabinet and threw more vodka down her throat. The guys nodded slowly.

'Then she's the boss … and you are working for the Russians.'

'No.' HH looked at Alexandra and smiled. She didn't return smile back but h seemed undeterred. 'But she's official; and one of us. British passport, Offic Secrets Act; the works.'

It took me a few more seconds to put it all together.

Nathalie …'

The boss.' HH sat again.

n case you have of interest' Alexandra said, pouring more drink 'Is of two. ame as yesterday, but this time they make trouble.'

Gone?' HH asked.

Gone.' She scowled at me and added 'For now.'

They laid it out for me. The bloke I had been sent to steal from really was in ahoots with the Russians, and so was the bloke who'd hired me. I was a awn in some game that really did involve the Russians and secrets. The oke had turned the girl, they told me. Now the Russians had both and they ere trying to mop up, which meant bumping me off.

They plied me with more booze and told me that we had to wait for further structions from Nathalie. I felt a little safer. I actually tried to make small talk ith Alexandra, who has the biggest, deepest blue – actually, they're violet – es I have ever seen. I thought that day she was the most beautiful girl I'd ver seen. But I hadn't yet seen Sally.

didn't jump the next time the door opened. Too drunk I suppose.

athalie strode in, slammed the door and surveyed the room. 'Bloody ussians!' She didn't seem to care about Alexandra being there and exandra didn't seem to care about Nathalie's remark. Everybody drank ore as Nathalie fired questions and everybody, including me, answered.

loody hell!' Nathalie threw her ski jacket on a chair and put hands on hips as e regarded me with annoyance. I felt like a school boy who had committed terrible infraction of the rules and was being considered for punishment by outraged mother.

really wish you wouldn't do this!' She was looking at TM.

on't blame me boss!' TM sounded offended. 'It's not my fault he went umping around in his size fourteen boots!'

e really can't have civilians messing things up like this!' Nathalie wasn't ppy and had no problem showing it.

ouldn't very well leave him to fend for himself' HH said calmly.

problem of his own!' Alxandra barked with a dramatic gesture.

ok' I began pathetically 'it really wasn't my …'

'Yes it bloody well was!' Nathalie's eyes were like emerald beacons that fixed me in their twin beams and almost blinded me.

'Little boys' Alexandra said darkly 'shouldn't play of big boy games.'

Eventually it was decided. Someone called Sally was arriving later that day. She was obviously essential to their plans but I had no idea why. I would be guarded like a boy who could not be trusted to walk around alone without getting into trouble. Nathalie seemed to deeply resent the responsibility of making sure civilians like me who got in the way didn't lose their lives but she seemed sincere about accepting the burden, for which I was grateful.

TM was to meet Sally at the airport and I was to go with him to be minded. HH and Nathalie would follow us in another car and it was felt this would afford protection on the journey. Anyway, most of it was in public places so the likelihood of any attempt at killing was thought low. At some point TM muttered 'Unless of course they've got a Sally' which meant nothing to me. I thought perhaps it was code for some kind of special weapon. I was only half wrong.

*   *   *   *   *

I'd sobered and cleaned up and was feeling confident. I am not without reserves, and I drew on them. Shaved, showered and dressed in my best clothes (one of the blokes had fetched my things from the hotel) I stopped being the naughty little boy and actually attempted to flirt with Nathalie (bad mistake) and Alexandra (*very, very* bad mistake indeed). They made me feel absolutely pathetic and I was more embarrassed than I'd ever been in my life. I stuck with playing the role of tough intrepid adventurer with TM.

'So' I said as TM piloted the black Mercedes to the airport. 'Who is this Sally? Is she like Nathalie?'

'Nope.'

'Alexandra?'

'Nope.' He was obviously amused.

'Does she work for British Intelligence?'

'No. She works for Nathalie.'

'Same as you and HH?'

'Kind of.'

'Like casuals?'

'We are not...' he sounded very annoyed '...casual about anything. We are specialists in our chosen field.'

'Which is?'

'It varies.'

'What's Sally's speciality?'

'Let's hope you never find out.'

With the sun shining over the trees and mountains around the airport I waited with TM for the arrival of Sally Twitchett. Elsewhere, Nathalie and HH watched for signs of trouble. I didn't know where Alexandra was but I assumed she was watching the lodge.

'It must be pretty difficult' I started, making conversation when none was needed. 'Working with those two.'

'Which two?'

'Nathalie and Alexandra.'

'Oh? Why?'

'God! They're absolutely gorgeous! Surely you noticed.'

'Yes. I noticed. But there are other things at stake in the field.'

'Do you see each other when, you know, you're off duty as it were?'

'No.'

'Shame.'

'What?'

'You don't see each other when you're off duty.'

'We're never off duty. Here's her plane.'

M led the way and we waited close to the arrivals gate.

'What does she look like?' I asked vaguely.

'You'll notice her; she's ... special.' TM smiled and I knew he was thinking something I would never get.

First impressions are important to me although I usually amend them as I get to know someone. The impact of my first impression of Sally never left me.

Sally Twitchett is five feet eight inches tall and she is very slim, which makes her look even taller. Slight would be a good word for it, but I later found out that her figure belied her speed and abilities. I've always gone for slim girls. Sally is that and more. Not super thin like Twiggy (I know she's still only seventeen and will probably put on a bit of weight as she gets older) but slimmer than most. And she is absolutely beautiful.

Sally's hair is the most incredible natural golden blonde you have ever seen and she wears it flowing around her shoulders. Her eyes are enormous hazel gems shaded by the longest eyelashes I've ever seen (and they're real). When she walks it's with an unhurried, graceful style a model would use in a fashion show: hips slightly forward, chin up, putting heel of one foot to toes of the other. Her make-up is always perfect, as are her fingernails, and she wears Paco Rabanne and Pucci as everyday clothes. Her legs go on forever and her arms are long and graceful, with the longest fingers unadorned by rings. Jewellery is always minimal, but perfectly chosen and of the highest quality. And Sally's skin would be the envy of any woman.

I actually caught my breath. *Special* was totally inadequate. Nathalie had impressed me as probably the most gorgeous girl I'd ever seen, but that went out the window as soon as I set eyes on Sally.

'Here comes Sally' TM said but I didn't need him to.

It didn't take long for Sally to clear Customs and her very short Paco Rabanne mini dress of silver plastic rectangles attracted a lot of attention, even under the long multi-coloured coat she left open. Gstaad airport attracts a lot of rich beautiful people but Sally Twitchett shone in Technicolor while everyone around her seemed to be in grainy black and white.

There were no words exchanged as we walked to the car park and Sally seemed totally oblivious to my presence, or perhaps she was deliberately ignoring me. TM smiled at her and she stared straight through him although he didn't seem to care. She walked in a cloud of what I discovered was Chanel Number Five and I couldn't take my eyes off her.

Nathalie and HH left before us, speeding off to tend to some unspoken business so TM and I had a good look around before getting in the car. Sally seemed completely oblivious to any possible threat and jumped in without a glance when I opened the door for her. She arranged herself elegantly on the rear seat while I tried not to stare at her endless legs as I closed the door.

TM started to drive and I half turned and started to introduce myself but Sally broke in as if I wasn't there. The first time I heard her speak it was a bit of a shock. Her voice is calm, soft, with a wonderful tone (I heard her sing in the shower once; she could be a professional) but sometimes it's with a very pronounced London accent some might call common. That's what I got the first time I heard her speak.

'I 'ope the Guv'nor knows what she's doing.' Sally looked out of the window as she said it; I saw because I had adjusted the rear view mirror so that I could see her. TM counter-adjusted it with a disapproving noise.

'Everything's in hand. How was your flight?'

'Terrible. No Krug or anything decent. Only Veuve Clicquot.'

'Yellow label I hope?' TM sounded genuinely interested and I wondered why the champagne on the flight was more interesting than whether anyone might be getting ready to kill us.

'Yeah. Some plonker kept tryin' to be sick. I asked for 'im to be put out of First Class but the stewardess seemed to want to play nursie with 'im.'

'What did they do with him?'

'Nothing. When he got up I pushed him in the loo and fixed the door so's it wouldn't open again. Rest of the flight was fine.'

'Didn't he make a fuss?'

'Don't be stupid darling! I fixed him!'

Sally's sudden change to a more sophisticated and refined style of speech threw me. It didn't seem to surprise TM and I wondered if she was prone to playing with accents. I learnt this wasn't the case and that she would use either style at length or for short periods of time, and alternating between them seemed perfectly natural.

'Good. We didn't spot any of the opposition so we should be okay.'

'Never mind that. Has Moscow got any decent clothes here?'

I assumed Sally was referring to Alexandra and soon learnt Sally called her nothing else.

'Same as usual.'

'Bloody 'ell.'

I was becoming more confused by the moment. Here was the most stunning girl I'd ever met who couldn't seem to decide how to speak from one sentence to another and who must be used to anticipating trouble; yet she seemed more interested in the champagne available on her flight and what her colleague was wearing than any danger we might be in.

'Well, there are some good shops in Gstaad, although I doubt they'll have anything that's up to date. I'll try to get her to …'

TM put the wheel over hard to the right but it was too late. The white Citroën Safari estate with the snow chains caught us on the left side and put us up on the snowy bank where we came to a halt. Ahead the Citroën turned and started back towards us and I could see a gun glinting out of a window.

I don't know why I turned around. I suppose I was concerned about Sally. What I saw bewildered me.

Sally wound down the window beside her, and there was suddenly a silver-plated Colt .45 automatic in each of her hands as she practically threw herself through the window and fired.

I turned back to see the Citroën lurch off the road and then span again in time to see Sally slide back in. The guns were nowhere to be seen but the bag beside her had moved. She stared at me with those huge hazel pools and then snapped 'What!? and immediately turned to TM. 'Bloody' 'ell! I've only been 'ere five minutes. Who were they?'

'Russians. Or maybe Sir Bertrand's.' He pulled the Mercedes back onto the road. As we passed the Citroën I saw the blood-splattered windscreen and the two bodies inside.

'My God' I muttered several times. 'My God you … you just …'

Behind me I felt Sally's warm sweet breath and that wonderful smell of Chanel and a warm summer night she always has. 'It's all right. Don't panic. You're safe.'

'But they might have … they might have got you …'

'Never a chance' TM said bluntly. 'She's too quick, you see.'

I turned and looked at Sally. She beamed and a shiver ran down my spine. She crossed and re-crossed her fabulous legs and said 'You must tell me all about yourself later. I'm Sally, but never Sal. I'm really looking forward to spending some time in Switzerland again. Do you come here much?'

It was as if she were chatting me up at a party or during treading in at a polo match. But somehow the combination of her voice, her fabulous looks, that smile and those eyes almost made me forget I'd yet again been saved by someone who didn't know me at all. Yet she hardly seemed to be attached to the same world in which it had happened and fascinated as I was, that unnerved me.

Sally was very nice to me for a few more minutes and then fell silent again and stared out of the window, ignoring me. I tried to make conversation but stopped when TM snapped at me.

Close your mouth and your ears for a few minutes. I need to speak with Sally about business.'

I got the impression TM wasn't keen on me speaking to Sally.

I honestly don't remember what they talked about. Half of it seemed to be in shorthand they'd clearly developed over a long time and I wondered about the nature of their relationship.

When we walked through the door of the lodge, Alexandra Krosova was by the drinks cabinet with a large glass of red wine in her right hand. She was dressed much as she had been the last time I saw her and looked a little dishevelled but nonetheless stunning.

'Bleedin' 'ell Moscow' Sally laughed as she strolled in 'you look like my aunt Mavis!'

'You have no aunt' Alexandra said darkly 'and always you make same silly jokes!' I was to learn with time that Sally was highly critical of the manner in which Alexandra dressed. This was not untidy or in poor taste. She chose clothes that were usually of dark colours and all were loose and often gypsy-style. Alexandra's hair was hauntingly thick and like the blackest silk, but it could have benefited from a professional cut. She clearly didn't feel the need to compete with the other women.

The contrast between Sally and Alexandra was striking but they were both magnificent in their own ways. As I got to know them better I saw how their relationship highlighted the way in which Sally would hold even the most serious of situations in contempt.

'At least it all matches!' Sally threw off her coat and stood by the fire. She looked amazing and I couldn't help but stare. I could feel the tension in the room and wondered what sparks would fly next.

'Now' Sally said as she accepted a large glass of wine from HH 'who the bleedin' 'ell *is* this plonker?' She didn't even look at me and I wondered if it was a tactic to keep me on edge.

H laid it all out for Sally, who sat on the club fender to the left of the fire, crossed her legs and stole my heart.

I noticed TM watching me. He did not look pleased and I wondered again about his relationship with Sally. This feeling grew as the days passed and I watched him as he looked at her when he thought she wouldn't notice. His eyes would light up. Sometimes Sally would behave as if they were some kind of long-term item. They were easy with each other and seemed in tune, though I never saw them touch each other. It seemed usual practice for her to ask him to make her a drink or just hold out her glass and he would jump to fill it. She would say things to him that suggested they had a relationship beyond work and as if nobody else was around:

You are THE most thoughtful, lovely man

Darling, make me a vodka martini would you? Nobody does it better

Which dress? The yellow or green?

When this is over you can buy me the most expensive dinner

I can't let anything happen to my little soldier. Leave it to me darling

'Fine.' Sally stood, held out her empty glass, which TM took quickly and refilled. 'If he gets killed that's his fault. And where's the Guv'nor?'

'Doing some shopping' HH said with a grin. He consulted his watch. 'She should be here in about ten minutes.'

'Then what?' I asked, tired of being ignored and made to feel small.

'We talk' Sally Twitchett said 'and you bloody well listen.'

*　　*　　*　　*　　*

Everything about Nathalie Endeavour, to give her full name, spoke of authority, confidence and strength. She came across as short-tempered, formidable, fierce and at regular intervals just bloody rude, which belied her undeniable gorgeousness. But there was obviously something else underneath. She and the others were clearly comfortable and familiar with each other to the degree that it was like watching a well-oiled machine at work.

They told me what I needed to know, and Nathalie made it absolutely clear that what she referred to as my *"Schoolboy adventuring"* had jeopardised the success of their current mission. They really were On Her Majesty's Secret Service and I had got in the way. I had become a target and a hindrance and they had to deal with both. My life was very much in their hands and I would be eliminated – Nathalie's word – very quickly if I did not do exactly as I was told. I was an inconvenience, but it was clear that Nathalie really did care about the lives of innocent civilians, meaning me. And she cared about the lives of the others. Several times she dismissed suggestions from them as she felt the risks involved were too great.

Over and over again I was sworn to secrecy. The circumstances, which I was told had partly been created by my blundering, demanded I be made privy to much that I shouldn't be.

ally played with me. At times she would flash me the most incredible smile
nd flutter those magnificent eyelashes, crossing and uncrossing her legs
hile I tried not to turn red; at others she ignored me or snapped either at or
bout me in her more common voice. But it didn't matter. I couldn't and didn't
ant to stop her consuming me. I even told myself that she may well be a
chizophrenic who took killing in her stride, but it didn't matter. That itself
became part of her fascination.

ust as I had speculated on TM's relationship with Sally, I began to wonder
bout Alexandra and the big bloke, HH. He wasn't as moody about it as TM,
ut I saw him glancing occasionally at the Russian as she moved around the
om, and his eyes were bright. If she noticed, she clearly didn't give a damn
nd I have to say I'd wish good luck to any bloke who fancied his chances
ith her.

exandra intrigued me. Apart from her spectacular looks (I couldn't help but
a little weak at the knees when I contemplated what she looked like under
ose long, loose clothes) she seemed angry much of the time. I knew there
as more to her. When she entered the lodge that day with the gun in her
ind and I thought she was going to kill me, she seemed cold, hard; yet
inutes later she had been angry that I hadn't been told all I should.

e blokes were more straightforward, or so I thought. TM was a bit of a
ndy. He cared about his appearance to a ridiculous degree and I reckon he
uld turn nasty about something as trivial as a spilt drink if it affected the way
looked. He looked like a movie star but I had no doubt he could be vicious
a tussle and wouldn't lose. And he carried knives. I saw him checking them
several occasions. A gun was sometimes in a shoulder holster, a small
tomatic which Sally mocked continuously.

H was a decent bloke I decided. Straight, clear about who he was and what
was doing. He'd made Sergeant in the Royal Marines, which meant he
as formidable. He also dressed immaculately, but more practically than TM
d in the classic way of a gentleman. Slacks, blazers, roll neck sweaters,
lished shoes, or suits, white shirts and ties; nothing fancy and all of high
ality.

new that I was in way over my head. And, although it was wrapped up as
otection, I also knew that I was a prisoner. They weren't going to let me
se and risk my getting in their way. Or was there another reason? My
agination was working overtime. And at any minute shots could start flying
ound and I could end up dead.

thalie didn't seem to care about keeping things from me. She engaged with
others in open discussion about what was going on. There were people
y wanted to flush out, people mixed up with Russians and bent Englishmen
o were in league with them. There were documents they wanted and film.

I stayed in the lodge for another three days, while the others, in various permutations, went and returned after an hour, sometimes several.

Nobody cooked much except me, and never the women except when Alexandra made endless slices of toast but there was a lot of drinking and, if I'm honest, I was half cut for most of it all. Sally seemed to treat the whole thing as a bit of a holiday and declared most days that she had no idea why she was there. When it was pointed out to her that she might at any time be needed to dispose of the opposition, as it was tactfully put, she shrugged and busied herself with criticism of shops or what was featured in the piles of fashion magazines she pored over every day. TM told me that whatever I thought I should rest assured that having Sally around significantly reduced the odds of anything bad happening. He told me that she was an incredible shot and that she never missed and that she had a sixth sense for such things. 'She can feel trouble before you can see it' he said.

As the days wore on Sally tried to find out as much about me as she could. I don't know why, even to this day. In between ignoring me and turning on the charm – or perhaps it was the coldness she turned on – she would smile, ask me questions and listen attentively as I talked. I was utterly bewitched, and she knew it. In fact, she had probably set out to do it from the minute I met her. I'm still trying to figure out why. But I believed it was because she was – is – genuinely interested in me.

After I had babbled meaninglessly one evening, Sally plied me with the best white Burgundy I'd ever drunk and said 'Why do you behave like such a plonker? Tell me something genuine about yourself. Tell me about one of your adventures. You must have done other things before you got mixed up in all this. What brought you here?'

I forgot that Sally hadn't been around when I'd gone through my past for the benefit of the others. So I told her pretty much my entire life story. At least it must have been most of it, because we got through three bottles of that fine Burgundy. I made much of my success during National Service, trying to impress upon Sally that I wasn't some kind of pathetic wimp and that I could actually handle myself. She wasn't impressed.

When I got to Marina's story Sally, who by that time had laid down on the rug by the fire next to me and stretched out her impossibly long legs, looked at me with those huge eyes and said 'That was a nice thing to do. That was the *right* thing to do.'

I showed mock indignation. 'What … did you think I'm totally without scruples?'

'No. I'm not sure who you are yet. But it was the right thing to do.'

'They've left you in charge of me, haven't they?'

Have they?'

I heard the back door. They're conspicuous by their absence.'

You're safe.'

I tried to laugh. 'That's debatable.' I meant with such a wonderful girl beside me, but if she got it she didn't show it. She just magically produced one of the silver .45 automatics.

How do you do that?'

She made the gun disappear again as if she were blowing out a candle.

Circus tricks. Now – get more wine from the fridge and tell me more about who you really are.'

So I did, and tried desperately not to force it or to sound as if I were trying too hard.

When I thought I had talked enough about myself I asked her 'And what about you? Tell me the story of Sally Twitchett.'

Her mood changed and I saw in her eyes that she was struggling with how to respond.

There's not a story that can be told.' She smiled warmly but I could tell her thoughts were somewhere a long way away and a long time ago.

There must be something to tell.' I smiled back.

Sally paused as she lifted the glass and it hung in the air, firelight reflected in but there was no way it could compete with the golden lustre of her hair. Then she said:

I didn't say there was nothing *to* be told; I said there's nothing that *can* be told.'

      *   *   *   *   *

I don't understand.'

It's not of your business!' Alexandra was clearly upset. She tried to pretend I wasn't in the room and started again on the plan she had been repeating for the past few minutes.

No. It's too dangerous. I won't risk another of you.' Nathalie was standing, hands on hips, facing the Russian who pounded her thighs with her fists in frustration.

'Sooka sin!' (Which I would later learn is Russian for *"Son of a bitch"*, one of Alexandra's favourite expressions).

Sally watched, unusually quiet as Alexandra turned away from Nathalie and poured more vodka.

'Will somebody please tell me what's happening? I'm not a naughty schoolboy and I won't go to my bedroom' I said petulantly.

'You'll do as you're bloody well told!' Nathalie was angry. I muttered something about being kept locked up for their purposes but still having to deal with everything and not being a kid and why didn't they trust me.

Sally walked slowly until she stood beside me, her arms folded across her chest. 'TM's missing' she said flatly as she searched my eyes.

'Is of five hours!' Alexandra added.

'And' Sally added flippantly as she crossed to the drinks cabinet and started to pour 'Moscow 'ere reckons we should split up and go and look for 'im.'

'Which is not going to happen' Nathalie said emphatically.

'Plonker's probably chatting up some dolly bird or gone shoppin' for cuff links.'

I was surprised by Sally's attitude, but I would learn that it was just another game, another curtain behind which she sometimes had to hide.

'Chyort!' from Alexandra. *

'Well' HH said, getting up slowly from his chair. 'We've got to do something. I' go.'

'I haven't decided yet' Nathalie said firmly, but I could tell from the way she and HH were looking at each other that she would acquiesce. 'Where would you start?' she asked.

'Last place we knew he was.' HH was doing up the tie he had loosened.

'If you're worried about leaving me' I said in as strong a voice as I could muster 'don't be. He saved my life and I won't have his compromised because of me. I'll go with one of you and help. I can handle a gun. Don't forget my national service. And I can handle myself if I'm ready.'

'You don't understand' Nathalie said, clearly annoyed.

* *Damn, hell!*

'Of course I do. He's either been taken by the Russians, or someone else, or …'

'Is bait!' Alexandra was staring at me, right hand on hip, the other making dramatic movements in the air. She seemed to think I was not getting something and looked at Sally.

'You're bait darling' Sally said as if it really didn't matter at all. 'They're supposed to come for you and then we take them and find out what we want. That's why you've been kept here.'

'Oh.' It was inadequate, but I couldn't think of anything else to say.

Sally added 'Didn't they tell you why you're so valuable? Apparently some of the microfilm we want to recover is hidden in the jewellery you stole. That's why Nathalie had TM and HH nick it from your hotel.'

I hadn't even checked the wretched jewellery since I'd been a captive.

Nathalie looked even angrier but kept quiet, possibly out of embarrassment but I doubt it.

When I recovered I said 'Oh' again and 'Well, thanks for bloody well telling me.'

'He's got a point.' Sally was standing next to me and her voice and manner had changed. She was more serious, concerned even. 'We used him. He's not the twit you might think. Here's an idea: I could take him with me.'

'Probably safest option.' HH said and looked at Nathalie.

'What is?' I asked dimly.

'Your best chance of staying alive is by being next to Sally' Nathalie said as if it were so obvious only a fool would fail to see.

'I'm glad you can see sense' said Sally and it was my first hint of how she wasn't afraid to challenge Nathalie, unlike the others.

'All right, all right!' Nathalie snapped. 'Take the bloody fool with you. I'll go to the hotel and you two…' she looked at Alexandra and HH and back '… go and find one of Promeko's little soldiers and make him talk.'

Alexandra was out the door first and didn't even bother getting a coat.

'Come on love!' Sally chirped at me. 'Let's go for a little drive in the country!' She sounded as if she were talking about a drive around Henley on Thames on a summer's day.

* * * * *

As Sally reached across me and pulled the radio receiver from the glove compartment she managed to bring the Maserati down from the reckless speed she'd reached and guide it to a stop. A white Mistral convertible, it had arrived two days previously. Sally had moaned much about the appalling delay in it being delivered. Apparently it only came from France where, of course, she keeps a residence. Snow chains had been fitted but I've never known anyone make a car go so fast on snow. That sixth sense TM spoke of seems to let her predict what's coming before it's there. It must be the same thing she has with guns.

I pondered as Sally drove me. She was she the most beautiful girl I'd ever seen, a mesmerising mixture of sophistication, humour, experience, insight and deadly skill. But who she really was … that perplexed me. I know enough about people … about women … to know the games they play. This was something completely different. Whoever Sally Twitchett was, you never saw the whole person at any one time. And there was sadness in her, hidden but always there. She often made inappropriate comments and at times refused to take danger seriously but she also had a sense of right and stood up to Nathalie and challenged her on my behalf.

It was exhilarating but at the same time rather scary. I'd been in some scrape and wasn't easily scared, but I'd never been exposed to death so many times Now I was riding into God knows what with Sally and who knew whether I or she would make it in one piece. She didn't seem to care.

'Can you read a map?' Sally had returned the receiver to the glove box.

'Of course I can.'

'Good. Then you are not without your uses.' Her voice had changed again. 'There are maps in a box in the boot. Get the relevant one.'

I jumped out and did as I was told. Sally gave me co-ordinates and I found the place straight away. It was only fourteen miles from us.

'Are we going to wait for the others?' I felt foolish asking because the look on Sally's face was outrage.

'Are you nuts!?'

The Maserati was flying before she looked back at the road.

The call had come from one of the others. They'd obviously got hold of *One Promeko's little soldiers* and he'd obviously spilled his guts. Possibly in more ways than one; I didn't ask and they didn't tell me.

As we drove, Sally told me that TM had been taken alive and was being held by Promeko in some old château close to the French border. Apparently the plan was to ransom him in exchange for me and the jewellery, which meant the microfilm.

And now Sally was driving me at ridiculous speed straight to them.

*　　*　　*　　*　　*

Sally had a rifle out of the car before it had stopped sliding. We were at the bottom of a long slope that led to the trees beyond which the château waited. I got out of the car as quickly as I could and went around to the boot where Sally was. In it was a small armoury.

'Give me a weapon' I said as calmly as I could.

'What for?' Sally looked at me with a bewildered look on her face. The absurdity of the scene didn't escape me. Sally was dressed, as usual, in a very short mini dress of bright swirling colours – I think this was by Pucci or Valentino – one of those – and white boots. She wore a long white coat, military style, and white tights. In her right hand was a rifle and in her left one of her beloved silver plated .45 automatics. She was beautiful and ready to kill.

I said, what the bloody 'ell do you want a gun for?'

'You don't think I'm going to let you go in there alone do you? Besides, you're supposed to be protecting me.'

'Who said anything about going in? If you try to follow me I'll shoot you in the leg; that'll offer you protection! Stay here.'

I said 'Look. I can shoot. I did national service. I'm not an idiot - you said that yourself. I'll do as you tell me.'

Sally looked at me with exasperation and then snapped ' Bloody hell! Here.' She threw a wooden box at me and I almost dropped it.

'Do as I tell you' Sally said sternly. 'Don't try anything and don't move from here. If anything happens, let off three rounds quickly.'

Sally took off as I took the automatic out of its case. I was surprised she could run so fast in high heeled boots and I really fought to catch her up.

From somewhere an engine roared and a car approached. I had no idea if it was the others or the opposition but I wasn't hanging around to find out.

When I made the top of the slope and was into the trees, Sally's footprints disappeared.

I crouched down in the brush and snow. Beyond the trees the land was flat, covered in a white blanket, and beyond that a fairy-tale château with turrets and all. There was no sound and I couldn't see Sally anywhere. I wondered why she had gone against Nathalie's instructions and left me alone and used that as justification for not doing as Sally had told me.

I almost had time to recognise the sound before I went face down in the snow. A firm hand pushed down on the back of my neck and I saw the blue-grey barrel of a hand gun by my face. Then I smelt that cinnamon and honey.

When Alexandra stopped pushing my face into the snow I raised my head and got on my elbows. She was crouching beside me on my left, still dressed like a gypsy and without a jacket. Wherever she had come from she had come quickly. She thrust binoculars at me.

Along the side of the château, pushing themselves into the wall, were Nathalie and HH making their way towards the big bay windows close to the front.

But where was Sally? I said the words out loud.

Alexandra hissed I should shut up and took off like a bat out of hell through the trees. I tried to keep up and failed. Then she was gone too, rifle slung across her shoulder.

I looked through the binoculars again; Nathalie and HH were almost at the window. Armed men patrolled the front of the house. They looked relaxed, smoking and chatting with each other, probably confidant they would see anyone approaching before anyone could trouble them. I don't know how Nathalie and the big bloke had got as far as they had but it suggested this wasn't a tight operation.

I checked the gun in my right hand.

'If you think you're going to hit anything with that from this distance, you can forget it.' Sally's voice floated down from above me, soft and calm.

I looked up and searched the trees. Perched in one was Sally Twitchett, rifle in hands.

'And don't try to look up my skirt.'

Sally shot first, then I heard a second rifle that must have been Alexandra's from a few feet away.

The guards at the front of the house went down, clutching arms and legs. The girls weren't going for kill shots and their shooting was impressive. Such accuracy over such a distance was beyond most.

Through the binoculars I saw Nathalie and HH by the bay window. Sally fired several times and it fell to pieces and her colleagues went in.

Alexandra was suddenly running, zigzagging across the open land towards the château. Suicide. I saw men appear at windows and said something about Alexandra being a sitting duck.

Don't worry …' Sally fired several shots and the figures in the windows disappeared. Several more appeared but Sally dealt with each of them before they could get a shot at Alexandra, who reached the door unscathed.

Sally slipped from the tree and landed beside me. She smiled and said 'Stay here love' then turned and ran like blazes, firing as she did.

I wasn't going to do as I was told and took off after Sally as fast as I could. She went in after Alexandra while I was still fifty feet away.

There was sudden rapid fire from several weapons and it went on for what seemed like an age. Then everything went quiet.

I'm pretty fit, but by the time I reached the open doors I was panting. Inside seemed deserted and I went in, pulling that silly move you see in the movies, swinging left to right with the gun outstretched. Pointless. Go left and you're dead from the right and vice versa. But I was still standing.

I could hear voices. There was an exclamation from a male voice followed by a shout from a female.

A man in black and leather rocketed into the hallway and I started to aim. He threw himself into a corner behind a console bearing an enormous brass lamp. A bullet ricocheted off of it and the man cried out in pain and fell silent. When I turned, Sally was walking across the hall, rifle in one hand, automatic in the other. She must have fired at the lamp as the bloke threw himself down and the ricochet got him.

'Keep back.' She didn't look at me and kept walking. The Colt in her left hand swung one way and the rifle the other and when two men appeared at either end of the galleried landing above she got them both immediately. I don't think she even looked as she fired.

It was a defining moment in the way I viewed Sally Twitchett. She was calm and composed, not a hair out of place but she was holding serious weaponry and used it ruthlessly. I didn't know at the time whether she shot to kill, but I did know that if she intended people dead they would be. I later learnt she would usually opt for wounding which tempered my initial shock..

There was a dream-like quality to the whole thing and the incongruity of the beautiful Sally and the violence was striking. I had to admit later that I found it stimulating but there was also a tragedy to it. How had someone like Sally come to live in such a way, where killing and risking her life were a matter of fact activity like ordering perfume?

Again, I didn't do as Sally told me. I followed her to the threshold of open double doors. I saw several men lying on the floor, blood spoiling the antique carpets, and Nathalie was standing over a man who was pleading with her not to kill him. She asked him again where Promeko and TM were and he shook his head and held up bleeding hands.

I didn't see what happened next because the door in front of me was suddenly slammed against me and I staggered backwards. I smelt Alexandra's scent and heard a single shot.

It must have been only seconds that I stood alone in the hall, gun in hand. Just as they say in the novels, it seemed like ages. Then I heard voices behind me; one I recognised as HH's.

Nathalie, Sally and Alexandra came back into the hall side by side. Nathalie went straight for me, taking me down before I had the chance to even register what was happening. There were gunshots, I hit the floor and heard men cry out. By flooring me Nathalie had saved my life.

While I pulled myself together and started to get up I saw three men appear on the galleried landing from the right; HH was up there and put one of them over the banisters. He hit the marble floor a few feet away from me with a sickening crunch. Alexandra took down the other two with casual precision and disappeared with Nathalie.

When I was standing again I saw Sally perfectly still, rifle up, automatic pointing at the floor. She looked at me with a disappointed frown.

'I told you to keep back.'

I saw the guy behind her and raised my gun. Before I could squeeze the trigger Sally dropped, whirled and fired and the bloke went down. He had a knife but no gun and would have struggled to do damage from that distance. When Sally turned to me again there was a look of real pain on her face. 'Get out! I can't do this with you here! Get back to the car and wait there!' She took off after the others with a clatter of heels.

I walked outside and realised what had happened. I'd followed Sally because I wanted to make sure she was all right. Instead I'd almost got myself killed and Nathalie had to save me. As a consequence Sally was distracted and either hadn't noticed the guy behind her or was too caught up in something else to deal with him immediately. She'd seen me preparing to shoot and had snapped out of it but not quick enough to make a decision and she'd put him down when it probably hadn't been necessary. She'd made an error of udgement. I don't know if the bloke was dead; if so, it had been an unnecessary killing and she'd have the guilt of that. If I hadn't been there Sally would probably have sensed him behind her early enough to move out of harm's way and drop him with a shot in the leg. There was something about the look on her face as she stood there, as if she'd left the world of the moment and was in a different place.

was getting in the way and was a liability, an unwelcome distraction.

Before I could wallow in guilt and self pity I saw four men, running fast from the château to my left. They weren't looking behind them as they made the Land Rover and didn't see me.

There were shots again from inside.

looked at the green Jeep that stood a few yards away and as the Land Rover started away, ran to it. Mercifully, the keys were in the ignition and it had snow chains fitted to the tyres. I was starting the engine when Sally appeared, went down on one knee and aimed at the Land Rover; but it was already in the trees and even Sally Twitchett couldn't stop it.

started towards Sally. She saw me instantly and ran and threw herself in as I braked and slid. I don't know exactly what she was saying, but she was cursing under her breath and there was blood in several places on her dress.

Are you …?' I didn't get to finish.

Shut up and drive! If we don't stop them now we'll lose them for good.'

Did you find TM?'

Yes. He's OK. His pride is wounded, that's all.'

Is everyone OK? Are you OK?'

Yes, for God's sake! It's not my blood. Why the hell didn't you do as I told you!?'

wanted to help.'

Idiot! Alexandra was right.'

There wasn't anything to say to that and I was busy keeping the Jeep going. It was rough, but I coped.

What's the plan?' I know I sounded a twit and certainly felt one.

We're going to stop them. We've got what we came for but they can't get away. They're too much of a threat.'

I don't know what she'd learnt but I knew she meant that she was going to kill them. Sally and the others must have found something very bad.

'If I can force them to stop …' I said. I think I was trying to help her have to use less extreme methods.

'Fool! How are you going to do that? Just get me as close as you can. And do exactly as I tell you!'

There were four of them. Even with one driving those weren't good odds, even for Sally Twitchett.

I was struggling to keep up let alone gain on them.

'They're headed for rough ground. They probably have a helicopter on the way. Damn, can't you get me any closer!'

I put my foot down and almost lost it. We were on very rough ground now. I knew we were fairly high and we were close to the edge of cliffs and the terrain was treacherous.

Sally cried out in frustration and before I knew it was hanging out of the Jeep taking a shot. I took my eyes off the ground to look at her and hit a rock. We bounced as Sally fired and she nearly fell. She cursed as she hauled herself in but the Land Rover slowed and suddenly stopped. I don't know if by some miracle she'd damaged it but she wasn't going to waste the advantage.

Sally leapt out of the Jeep and raced for cover. Three men were out of the Land Rover already and she fired. She must have hit the fuel tank because the thing erupted. One bloke yelled and fell, trying to extinguish the flames that spread over him. Another dived for cover and Sally got the third before he could really move. The fourth bloke hadn't made it out at all.

I climbed out of the Jeep and took cover. Moments later I heard an aircraft and saw the helicopter approaching.

I waited for Sally to make a move. Around us the terrain fell sharply away in places. I couldn't tell how deep but it needed careful negotiation. I could see several deep cracks in the rock between Sally and the man behind cover. Sally would wait for him to make his move and then deal with him.

I could see the chap who'd been set alight when the fuel tank went up wasn't dead. He'd put out the flames and was getting up. I'm sure if he'd just made a run for it she would have let him go, but he turned and readied his gun in Sally's direction. There was a crack and he went down. I saw him moving, just.

I started to feel relief. There was just the bloke behind the rock. He'd have to break cover to fire and she'd have him. It was only a matter of time. I wasn't going to do anything stupid but stayed alert. I could see Sally plainly and thought she must be freezing. I later learnt she didn't let things like heat and the cold bother her.

When she did it I was horrified and couldn't understand what she was up to. Sally suddenly stood and walked calmly from cover and into the open. She had dropped the rifle and was holding the silver automatic in her right hand. She started to walk towards the guy behind the rock. Later I asked her why she did it, but she couldn't, or wouldn't tell me, simply saying *"It doesn't matter now."* Maybe she was fed up with waiting or perhaps she wanted to give him a chance.

I leapt up and wanted to shout but couldn't. I was terrified that I'd distract her. I saw the target lean out from behind the rock just as Sally seemed to fall through the earth beneath her. There was the sound of falling snow and stones and she was gone. There had been fresh snow and it had probably combined with leaves to obscure the opening and in any case Sally would have been focussed on the gunman. Had he known it was there? Was this why they'd come this way?

The helicopter was getting closer.

I pushed out of cover, gun up, firing repeatedly to keep him pinned down. Where Sally had fallen the land fell rapidly in all directions. She'd gone down a deep split in the rock, just wide enough for her and she was hanging on by one hand a few feet below me. As I flattened myself on the rock I heard the gunman's boots as he started to clamber towards us. We were partly obscured so he'd have to come quite close to get a shot but it wouldn't be long.

Sally was holding on to rock with her left hand. Beneath her was a drop of about twenty feet into darkness and about two and a half feet behind her but too low for her to reach was solid rock and earth again.

I reached down and just about managed to grab her left wrist; her other arm was hanging limp and was clearly injured but I still said 'Give me your other hand.'

'Can't. It's hurt.' She sounded ridiculously calm. Sounds came steadily on.

Sally said 'He's coming. Leave me; he'll kill you.' She'd dropped her gun and thrown mine down in my panic to save her. I had both my hands around her thin wrist and even with the immediate threat was struck by how little she weighed. I tried to swing her up but she cried out immediately and told me her foot was trapped as she struggled to work it loose.

'He'll kill you and the other one's not dead. Make a break for it while you have time.'

It was her eyes that got me. They told me she was resigned to whatever might happen.

'Please … let me go. Save yourself.'

She wasn't helping me and had stopped trying to free her foot. I didn't get it. 'Hold on … I'll pull you free' I said but she shook her head frantically.

'No! You must go now!'

I couldn't pull Sally up because her foot was trapped. We didn't have time enough to do anything about that. If I let her go she might fall and if that happened she'd be badly injured or worse. My gun was maddeningly close but I wasn't sure I'd be able to reach it without letting go of Sally.

I let go of Sally with my left hand and started to stretch for the gun. I saw her shaking her head and her eyes were closed. In a small, pleading voice she said 'No … not again.'

It was suddenly too late to do anything.

'Leave it alone pal!' His voice was rough and there was pleasure in it. 'Kill yo huh? Yeah; dead right I'll kill you. Then I'll finish her off, the bitch!'

I actually had a plan. I'd lie still, let him come closer. He'd be the sort to want to gloat before he did it. With any luck I could get him down before he did for me. Sally might just pull herself up and reach the gun and …

After the bullet made a hole in his forehead he stood there for a moment with a blank stare then crumpled. The second shot got the wounded guy who'd somehow hobbled to join his mate.

I didn't process what had happened. I just grabbed Sally's arm with both hands again and pulled. I don't know whether she'd freed her foot herself or yanked her free but it was only seconds before she was standing next to me looking back the way we'd come. I saw Alexandra, rifle still in her hands, running towards us with Nathalie close behind and I thanked God for the Russian.

The sound of the helicopter filled the air and the shots started. We all darted for cover. Sally seemed largely unharmed apart from her right arm but the leather of her boot was torn and I could see blood.

The helicopter hung above us. If we moved we'd be picked off easily. If we didn't we'd be trapped and all they had to do was land and come after us. I don't know how many men they had, but it was a big helicopter and the fire was coming from several weapons.

We wouldn't be able to do anything much with hand guns; Alexandra would have to do something with the rifle.

I watched Alexandra prepare to take a shot and I got the second big surprise of the day. She suddenly lowered the rifle and tossed it to Sally who caught it with her left hand, twirled and laid it across my right shoulder as she kneed me into the right position.

HH and TM arrived and started firing at the 'copter to provide a distraction.

One shot. I don't know what it hit but it did the job. The helicopter dipped left then right and started to twirl. That's when Sally walked out into the open and shot off three more shots one-handed (you'd think she was in a Western). The helicopter dipped out of sight. There was a loud bang and black smoke, followed by a small explosion. Things don't always erupt spectacularly the way they do in the movies.

Sally tossed the rifle at Alexandra. As she walked past her she muttered 'Sight's off. I'll fix it later.' She was limping slightly, must have been freezing cold but didn't seem to give a damn.

*   *   *   *   *

Sally was odd, although I wasn't sure what I'd expected. She hadn't said a word to me since the helicopter went down. She travelled back with TM and HH drove me in a hired Merc. He didn't say much and I rambled on a bit. He basically told me things turned out okay, we all made it, and the job had been done. He was clear I needed to keep my mouth shut and do what I was told.

I apologised to Sally several times. The first time she listened without a word and I really didn't like the sadness in her eyes as she did. The other times she just literally turned her back on me.

Turned out Sally had torn tendons and a strained muscle in her arm. She refused to see a doctor at first, saying that her self-diagnoses were always correct but TM went on and on at her until she agreed to let him take her to see a doctor. When she came back she drank bucketfuls of the champagne they'd picked up and chatted about absolutely nothing or fell into a long silence. Nobody seemed to find this odd but she was clearly ignoring me and avoiding any talk whatsoever about what had happened.

HH told me that he didn't know who'd checked, but the bloke without a gun Sally put down was still alive when people went in to clean up. I was pleased, but she didn't say a thing or show any emotion when he told her.

I wondered who cleans up after a gunfight and carts off the bodies. HH told me 'We have people.'

Nathalie was pretty harsh with me. She kept it up for over an hour. After about ten minutes I stopped trying to interrupt, defend myself, or argue. There was absolutely no point.

The beautiful chestnut haired secret agent made it absolutely clear to me how many dozens of opportunities there had been for me to muck up her operation, and get people - including myself - killed. She must have realized that I was beginning to find it amusing, because at some point towards the end she started talking like a middle-class middle-aged aunt whose nephew had gone out on a bender and not fetched up until seven thirty the next morning. Then she pulled out a copy of the Official Secrets Act and made it clear that I was to sign it and that if I ever said a word about any of this to anyone I would suffer dire and severe consequences.

I signed gladly.

TM was fine. Took a bit of a hammering, but by his account the blokes who did it got a few knocks in the process and anyway, they're dead now. He was very concerned about finding a decent place to get his hair trimmed. We drank a lot and he was quite complimentary about my part in things, which he had heard from HH and possibly Nathalie. Sally I wasn't sure about, but he knew that I had tried to save her. That obviously went a long way with him.

Alexandra was dark and brooding as ever, but she and Sally exchanged words several times in low voices out of everybody else's earshot, another thing that surprised me because I thought there was no love lost between them.

I saw TM looking at Sally often and he made no attempt to cover it up. If they'd had any kind of relationship other than colleagues and perhaps friend it would have shown. It didn't.

HH told me that I should stick around until Nathalie decided I wouldn't be needed. They also wanted to make absolutely sure there weren't any of Promeko's men left around to cause trouble. I suggested I go back to my ho but TM told me with a smile that my bill had been paid and anyway, the lodg was big enough and paid for so why not enjoy it for a few days?

So I stayed put for another couple of days. I asked Sally one evening if I'd really upset her and apologised again. This time she looked at me and said 'It's just me. You don't need to apologise. It's done; over with.' She smiled a put a hand on my cheek but took it away when I put my hand over hers.

'What happens now?' I asked when we were all drinking again and I was tire of waiting for someone to tell me.

'Sally gets to rest up until she's healed' TM said.

...ally muttered something about deciding for herself what she would do and
...obody questioned her.

...he rest of us will go back' Nathalie said. She was a bit tipsy and less fierce
...an usual. I'd been told all was clear so everyone could relax.

...ack where?' I asked.

...ondon old chap.' HH smiled at me. 'What about you? Still going to head for
...ance?'

...I forgotten what a state I'd got myself into. TM had stuffed an envelope fat
...th French Francs into my pocket before all hell had broken loose. I was
...ven more embarrassed than before about taking his money.

...don't know' I said. 'I suppose I could. Or I could go back to London myself.' I
...dn't want to leave Sally alone and I got the impression some of them knew
...I suspected TM of watching when Sally put her hand on my face.

...exandra regarded Sally with an odd expression on her face. She looked at
...e several times and then said to Sally 'Why you not go to house of Brittany.'
...ne walked up to Sally who was sitting quietly by the fire and handed her a
...ass of brandy.

...ally stared into the fire. 'Why would I go there?'

... of best place. You have old man on farm and maid to come.'

...ave to admit Alexandra's concern for Sally surprised me, rough-edged as it
...as, but Sally seemed to cheer at the thought. With hindsight I think
...exandra knew mentioning it would have a positive effect but I had no idea
...at it would all ultimately mean.

...nat's a good idea' TM said enthusiastically. 'You haven't been back there for
...ong time.'

...) ... no, I suppose I haven't.'

... check out flights for you' TM said.

...n - oh, I couldn't possibly stand the thought of another ghastly flight.'

...ell, you can't drive' HH said. 'Not with a damaged wing.'

... e doctor said I might be fine in a few days.'

...en wait' I said, desperately hoping for an opportunity to stay with her.

Alexandra turned and paced a semi-circle around me with what I almost thought was a mischievous look on her face. It was the first time she'd looked at me without scowling. Then she exclaimed dramatically 'Take foolish boy! He has nothing to do! He can drive you.'

You could have knocked me over with a feather.

'What are you playing at, Moscow?' Sally was looking at me as if she'd never seen me before.

'I'd be glad to' I offered eagerly. 'And I'd appreciate the lift. I might enjoy France after all.'

'Is of two stones for bird.'

'Two birds with one stone' HH said gently. It was his habit to correct Alexandra's English, which nobody else, not even Sally, ever did and Alexandra never objected.

'Is of same thing' the Russian said as she watched my reaction.

'It makes sense' Nathalie said, suddenly not sounding drunk at all. 'I need everybody else back in London with me. You need a break, Sally. And fit. I may need you again soon.'

'How terribly kind.' Sally said.

'You can make sure this twit gets out of here in one piece.'

'I thought you said it was all clear?' I said.

'Hah! In this business you can never relax!' Nathalie seemed to delight in reintroducing the idea that I still might not be safe.

'But she's injured!' I said, annoyed.

'She's better with one arm than any of us with two and certainly better than you' Nathalie said.

'That' Sally said 'is very true. Perhaps it's not such a daft idea.'

'And you can at last help by getting her out of here.' Nathalie picked up a small but expensive leather bag and threw it at me. 'There. I got your nickel jewellery and bonds dealt with after we got what we wanted. They converted into something that should be more useful to you.'

I looked in the bag. It was full of money. I stupidly said I couldn't accept it.

Call it conscience money.' Nathalie put on a coat and said she was going back to the hotel. 'I want to get out of this bloody village and back to civilisation! I'll see the rest of you at the Palace in an hour. Don't be late.'

I told TM I'd give him back his money. He didn't seem bothered. Whereas he'd been enthusiastic about Sally going to Brittany earlier he didn't seem very pleased now.

'What will you do after you deliver Sally?' he asked me pointedly.

'I don't know' I said. 'Possibly try Paris for a while.'

In a sudden change of mood Sally jumped up and said cheerily 'Don't worry TM! I'll sort 'im out.'

'Is time for us to go' Alexandra said to HH, even 'though it was only a fifteen minute drive to the hotel. The big man took the hint straight away.

Sally was wearing a very short finely knitted orange dress with a black collar and tie pattern in the fabric and looked gorgeous and suddenly mischievous. She stood in front of me with a curious expression on her face. 'Well then matey - looks like I'm lumbered with you. Let's hope you've got enough in that little bag to pay for decent meals on the way.'

'That's settled then' I said because I couldn't think of anything else. I was suddenly loaded and looking forward to travelling with Sally into France. Maybe things were going my way at last.

'Take care old man' HH said pleasantly as he walked past me. 'Hope things work out for you in the future. Maybe get a job in sales or something, eh?'

Alexandra stopped and fixed me with those amazing violet pools of hers. 'You will have of care' she said. 'Still much is at stake.'

I spluttered something like of course I would.

'Are you sure ...' TM asked Sally after Alexandra and HH had left.

Sally went to him and put her head on his chest. 'Yes. Yes, I think I am sure. But you're sweet for asking. He'll take care of me - won't you?'

'I thought Nathalie said it was the other way around' I said flippantly.

She looked at me and said quietly 'No. No ... it isn't.'

'Guv'nor's orders TM!' Sally said firmly. 'We don't muck about with the Guv'nor's orders, now do we?' She sounded refreshed and busied herself with making a drink. It was clearly a signal that TM was dismissed.

Then I was alone with the most wonderful girl in the world, whose state of mind was a complete mystery to me.

*   *   *   *   *

We decided to wait until morning before we set off. The lodge seemed very large without the others, in more ways than one.

Sally relaxed by the fire after packing and moaned about how few clothes sh had with her. We would absolutely have to stop in the village before we went as she needed some essentials if we were going to take it at a leisurely pace and perhaps stop overnight somewhere.

I was issued with a comprehensive list of instructions as to what I could and couldn't do, how to drive her Maserati, directions and so on. I was just thankful that she wasn't resisting the idea.

After talking to someone on a little radio Sally insisted we went down into the village to take dinner. It seemed like a different place. Sally had changed an she looked like an angel in a fur collared coat and hat. 'It's fake' she said when I whistled. 'I don't wear real fur. The animals don't get a say in it and that's not fair.'

A dress worth a hundred, probably and a bracelet, watch and earrings probably worth a thousand more. But with them she wore a hand tailored co and hat with fake fur. She had become warm and approachable and seeme to have relaxed into her more sophisticated style.

Evening and good food and wine brought a more relaxed mood but I kept looking around, anxious and wanting not to be.

'You look like Sean Connery in an out-take from a Bond film' Sally said with grin. 'Relax. There's no one around to hurt us. And we've got a guardian angel.'

'What?'

'From time to time we need someone from the service; sometimes two. Nathalie likes to keep a tight team, but we're only human. She left Uncle To behind.'

'Uncle Tom?'

She laughed. 'I hear Alexandra was called upon to come into the bar and convince you the Russians were after you.'

I thought for a moment and it dawned on me.

'es! I remember! When she came into the lodge that day when I was with TM nd HH I remembered her from the bar and thought my number was up! I ought she'd come to kill us.'

nd there was a chap she talked to in the bar. Remember?'

'es. Well; I don't remember much about him. Pretty anonymous looking oke actually.' I had been very drunk.

xactly. That's what Uncle Tom does. You never know he's there.'

ow did you know about that? You weren't here at the time.'

he boys told me.'

hey had me fooled, you know. Anyway …who pays for Uncle Tom's rvices?'

er Majesty.' Sally smiled again. She was smiling lots.

he really anyone's Uncle Tom?'

ourse not you silly plonker!'

e got so many things I want to ask you.'

now.' Sally looked serious for a moment. 'I haven't said thank you.'

here's no need. You would have done the same for me.'

e looked sad. 'I could have got you killed.'

ell you didn't. Anyway, I nearly did the same to you. Twice!'

. I knew I wasn't going to die. Not then. Not here.' She spoke as someone ed to contemplating her final moments. 'But you were prepared to die to ve me.'

I said - you would have done the same thing.'

was still very brave of you.' She looked away for a moment then said 'It esn't happen very often.'

at people try to save you? What about the rest of your firm?'

u make us sound like criminals! Of course they would - but it doesn't ppen often. It's usually me that has to look after them. I'm not used to being ked after.'

I kept my mouth shut because there were suddenly a hundred things I wanted to say but knew the time wasn't right.

We drank more champagne and then Sally seemed to cheer and said 'Well - we'll say no more about it then!'

'Do you mind if I ask you things?'

'Depends what things.' She leant forward and fluttered her eyebrows. 'I hope you're not going to ask me *naughty* things …'

'Why did you take me with you? It wasn't what Nathalie had planned, was it?'

'No. But I couldn't let the others go after TM without me. And I didn't want you too far away either. It seemed like the best solution.' She smiled. 'Besides' she said in a playful voice 'I figured you could handle yourself.'

'You were mad at me for not doing what you told me. That's why you didn't speak to me for …'

'No. I knew you would come after us. I knew you couldn't stay back. I'd hoped we'd get the job done before you got yourself hurt. And I wasn't … I wasn't mad with you.'

'I wasn't afraid. Not for myself. But I bloody well was for you. When you went down that rock face … well …'

She put her head in one hand.

'You poor man.' She wasn't being unkind. She really meant it. 'You really shouldn't be in this world, should you?'

'I don't understand Sally …'

'You're too nice.'

'Bah! I'm not sure about that!'

'I think I'd like to leave now.'

'Oh. Will Uncle Tom be coming with us?'

'No. Definitely not. But there will be people around, watching. Just in case. We won't have to shoot anybody tonight.'

Later in the lodge there was a big fire and brandy.

'What did you mean … when I was trying to pull you up?'

What do you mean?' I'd waited for what I thought was the right moment but I knew from her face there never would be one.

'You said … I was a bit distracted … but it was something like " Not again … No, not again."'

Sally looked into her glass then drained it.

'I'm sorry. I just wondered …'

'In my life' Sally began as she got up to get more brandy 'you learn not to get close to people. Not to worry about them. Unless you know they can fight their way out of whatever comes at them. Unless you know they're quite prepared to die at any moment. And it's important …' She paused for a moment. 'It's important to know that if someone does die … someone next to you, that you care about … that it's not your fault. They have to make a choice, you see, and accept the consequences.'

'I'm sorry …' I didn't have to think too hard to know that she'd lost someone and blamed herself.

Sally looked at me from the drinks cabinet she was leaning against. The firelight played in her hair and her eyes caught the flames and glittered. 'It was almost a year ago. He was an innocent fool who got in the way. I let him play his game and didn't send him away soon enough. And he got killed.'

'I'm sure it wasn't your fault …'

'No. It wasn't. But it might have been. And I thought you were going to be killed, and that really would have been my fault.'

'I won't let that happen.' I don't know why I thought that was appropriate but it worked and to my very great surprise, Sally picked up the decanter of brandy and came and lay beside me by the fire.

I asked a look at her legs and feet while she stared into the fire and noticed the bandage around her right foot.

'Does it hurt?' I asked without taking my eyes off her beautiful long feet.

'What?' Then she realised what I was talking about. 'Oh … no; no it doesn't hurt at all.'

'Was it really stuck in the rocks?'

'Shut up …'

I don't know who moved first. I've thought about it and I think she did. Anyway, that was when we kissed.

I tried not to kid myself. I was still very unsure about just who Sally Twitchett was and told myself I shouldn't depend on anything lasting. But it really was like being in heaven. Here I was with the most glamorous, beautiful girl in the world, driving her leisurely to her home in Brittany in a white Maserati with the top down despite the cold. I had enough money in that little leather case Nathalie had given me to make me feel as if I really was a rich man. Sally had said that the guy who'd hired me had been dealt with so there was nothing to worry about there.

Sally was a different girl. She laughed and smiled a lot, although there were times when she seemed distracted and melancholic. Her voice stayed the same - that refined style touched with laughter and a delight to listen to.

Several times the radio in the car had hummed and Sally spoke briefly. Then she sounded more like the girl I had first met. It was Nathalie, she had said, TM, or someone else checking to make sure she was still all right. Afterward it would take about twenty minutes for Sally to become herself again. It seemed she had to put aside that part of her life to focus on me. Then she would lean into me, head on my right shoulder as I drove. I didn't need to say anything, and the cold winds never touched us.

We crossed into France quickly and the sun was with us all the time as I took it easy. We used the back roads, the longest route. Sally was in no hurry to get home, she said, although she wanted to see her horse d'Artagnan. He lived in a field behind Sally's house and there was a barn he inhabited when he chose. He was very old but very *"Hoity"* – interesting word for a horse – and was looked after by an old Frenchman who owned the farm adjacent to Sally's land. This chap had been in the French Resistance and did various things for Sally very slowly, like watch the house when she was away, forward mail and other such important things.

The house wasn't what I had expected. For a start it was much larger and much grander than Sally had let on. It had been part of the inheritance she had received when her last remaining family member – an aunt who had little interest in her – had died.

The manoir (French for what English people would call a manor house) was big. Very early eighteenth century, I guessed, with a huge hall, rooms leading off it and a grand marble-floored corridor leading to the rear rooms and the most enormous kitchen I've ever seen. The hall featured a very grand staircase winding up to a galleried landing. There were paintings and sculptures and enormous potted plants (tended in Sally's absence by either the old chap next door, or the maid – another ancient French hero who must have been in her late sixties, possibly even her nineties) and the odd hanging tapestry. I never got to explore the house and we used only a handful of rooms.

here was no trace of the up-to-the-minute fashion-crazy Sally. Everything as old. All the furniture was antique and the wallpaper had been hand-painted in some long-forgotten era. Clean as the proverbial whistle, but old.

s I stood in the hall and looked around for the first time Sally said 'I know. It's a bit ancient and decrepit. I must decorate some day. But I just can't seem be bothered. And it seems to want to stay this way.'

on't you get lonely?'

lly looked at me as if I were bonkers. 'No, silly!. Never. Quick! Let's go and e d'Artagnan!'

vatched Sally run across the grass that was much too long, leap the rotting ket fence like an athlete and cross the field to the old chestnut brown horse anding in the corner of what served as a paddock. It was big enough to ve catered for a hundred horses. She fed d'Artagnan apples and carrots m the small bag she had thrown over her shoulder and she looked like a ild. Her golden hair shimmered in the brilliant Brittany sunshine and as I ned against a wall I wondered how such a beautiful creature had become xed up in such a horrible violent world. It already felt an age ago but it had en no time at all that we both could have been killed several times over.

r a few days I played spot the artist. I was quite good with art and antiques d I stopped keeping a tally of how much the contents of the house were rth after the first day. Sally would be very rich if she ever sold the house d its contents, but it was obvious that she regarded the whole thing as both annoyance and a place to be kept just as it was. Later I realised it was the t remaining link between her dead family and past and the world she now abited.

e gambled and I lost a packet and then won most of it back. It wasn't a long ve to the casino and hotel, but it was long enough for Sally to want to stay he hotel after each night's play. She was well known and the waiters and ff treated her like the magnificent woman she was. She dressed simply but ctacularly in tiny black numbers, forgoing the usual Rabanne and Pucci.

lly was the sophisticated woman she had shown me since we'd been left ne. This place seemed to be a haven for her where she could be who I eved was the real Sally Twitchett.

e first time I heard some maître d' address her as Miss Athelston-Twitchett I sn't that surprised. She looked and acted every inch the English Lady. I n't even have to ask.

a pseudonym' Sally said with a smile at dinner that evening.

at is? Sally Twitchett or Sarah Athelston-Twitchett?'

'That's for you to guess!'

Take your choice. Sally Twitchett; Sarah Athelston-Twitchett (the Honourable if you please, but that title's only used in written form and she never uses it). My money's on the Honourable Sarah. Sally Twitchett was like an alter-ego, I decided, the person who does the dangerous stuff and pretends it's all just a bit of fun.

It was like the best spy film ever made. The beautiful English lady with a tortured past, a match for any killer, with a life of adventure and life-threatening service to her country behind her, seeking to find true happiness with the slightly naïve handsome young Englishman who had fought through her defences.

But I knew it wouldn't last.

One day a telephone call came and Sally flew up the stairs to return minutes later with a slightly battered Louis Vuitton suitcase and a wooden case I knew contained weapons.

She paused only briefly in the hall, dressed in some Paco Rabanne space-age mini.

'Stay and do as you please' she said curtly. 'I'll see you when I see you.'

I tried to hold her and kiss her but she kept the gun case in the way.

'Bloody 'ell! I'm only off to London for a bit! Get a grip you silly thing!'

And then she was gone after giving me the lightest peck on the cheek.

I heard nothing, despite having called out for her to let me know she was all right. I contemplated following her but I knew that would be disastrous.

Sally returned eight days later. There was a cut on her right forearm and a graze on her right temple just under her wonderful hair. I didn't ask, but she saw me looking and said sharply: 'I ran into a branch.'

The running I could see, the branch was a lie. Sally has a sense of balance and everything around her; she never has accidents. She had also returned without any luggage. I actually thought that night of her return, when she was out cold as if she hadn't slept for the whole time she'd been away, of looking in her passport to see where she'd been. Had it really just been London?

I was exhausted myself; apart from the odd hour here and there, I hadn't slept while she'd been away. Each day, as if the place were deserted, the old Frenchman came in and checked the post and did his rounds. He passed me several times as if I was a ghost and I didn't interrupt his service. He seemed to have decided that it was his duty to check that Sally was all right and that the house was secure, although he never went upstairs without asking Sally

...st. One morning I got up at six. Sally was out cold and I took a look out of ...e huge window on the landing at the rear of the house. The old Frenchman ...as walking slowly along the perimeter, checking the fencing and looking ...round him. He looked up at me as if he'd sensed someone was looking down ...d I waved. He just walked on.

...e *"Maid"*, who I learned was called Veronique, came in every other day to ... things, although I had no idea what. She chastised me cruelly in common ...ench for not watering the huge potted plants in the hall. I tried to tell her that ...idn't want to take her job, but gave up. She was obviously deaf as a post.

...ese old French people didn't treat Sally as an employer and she never ...eated them as servants. They didn't do anything like washing, ironing or ...eaning. A young man came once a week to collect and deliver laundry. I had ... laugh when the deadly and spectacular Sally Twitchett pointed to a vast ...om and told me there were baskets and that my laundry should go in them. I ...so had to laugh when I saw her with a duster one day. She didn't ...derstand why her doing anything domesticated would make me laugh. I ...ked her where she kept the vacuum cleaner and she looked puzzled for a ...oment. Then she said she didn't know and explained that there was a girl ...o usually came and *whisked around the place* but that she had recently got ...arried and was on honeymoon. I asked where they'd gone and Sally told me ...e had arranged for them to *spend a few weeks in Rome - as a wedding ...esent.*

...id most of the cooking when we didn't go out to eat. Sally could make a ...asonable sandwich but only ever ate less than half and she wasn't bad at ...rambled eggs. These would always be accompanied, whatever the time of ...y, by pink champagne.

...hough she was always spectacular when we went out, when we were at ...e house Sally would not use makeup and dressed in jeans and a shirt a lot ...the time. She was still remarkably beautiful. She would wander outside ...refoot and not bother about walking grass or dirt into the house. This was in ...ch contrast to the other Sally I had experienced. Although at first puzzling, ...time passed and she remained the same I felt relieved and convinced that ...s was the real Sally, or Sarah.

...e second time Sally went away I was much more vigorous in my approach. ...e was different this time and actually tried to explain that this was what she ...and that I shouldn't worry. She would be with Nathalie, TM, HH and ...xandra. I thought it curious she didn't call Alexandra *"Moscow"* the way she ...to her face.

...u mustn't worry. It's a simple operation. There won't be any bad trouble. ...just there for insurance. I'll try to call from London, but I need to sort out ...thalie's boutique as well – terrible state with practically no stock and what ...re is just ...'

'Shut up!' I kissed her and held her and she told me to let her go before she passed out.

I did let her go and then said 'I'm coming with you.'

Sally's eyes grew dark and her face turned to stone.

'Don't ever do that again.'

'If it's a simple operation, why not?'

'I told you - don't ever do that again. I don't want you with me. Not when I'm working.'

That's all she said. She didn't need to say any more. I backed off. I was wounded and scared I'd gone too far.

'For God's sake be careful!' I called after her.

Sally skipped down the old stone steps to the waiting Maserati and called back 'I will!' like a teenage girl off on a trip for the first time. She threw me a wonderful smile and waved as she thundered away and I felt she'd forgiven me. But I'd learnt a lesson I didn't like.

That time it was over ten days and of course there was no 'phone call. And then the old Frenchman came into the dining room where I was staring at the Matisse over the fireplace and he handed me a postcard. A *postcard*, of all things, written in Sally's large swirling hand.

"Having wonderful time in London. The weather's lousy but we're all coping. Bit of a delay because the Queen is having a bit of a bash and we're invited. See you in a week.

141.5

Ta-ra

Love XXX

PS: Don't forget – explore the cellar"

The cellar was vaulted and half full of the best wines I had ever seen and barrels of old brandy. On one wall in a huge alcove – there were several, vaulted and high – was a display of a couple of dozen antique firearms. In another there were swords and lances and in another still, riding gear.

Why had Sally sent me down there? I opened a bottle of the best Burgundy and realised that a glass and corkscrew had already been laid out on a long oak table and recently as there was no dust. That number - 141.5 - had bee halked on the table next to the glass. Sally was playing a game. Or perhaps he was testing me?

explored as I drank and pondered the number. Then it clicked.

When I knew what I was probably looking for it didn't take long. I crawled round until I found the power cables and followed them. Brandy casks don't eed power cables and it took only minutes to find the right one.

he little doorway clicked open and the radio said hello. It was on and umming. I pulled out the earphones, donned them and listened. 141.5. Odd ing to put on a postcard, I had thought. But it meant megahertz. I tuned and stened. I actually flipped a switch and said *"Hello."* Nothing, but I noticed the tle tape recorder connected to the receiver and pressed the rewind button.

inished the bottle of wine and went for another. I opened it and pressed play ut there was no sound so I put the headphones back on.

here were two messages recorded.

ello darling. If you've found this then it means you're as clever as I thought. on't think badly of me for having a bit of fun!

an't telephone - it's not secure. We're okay but I'll be a while longer. This is unday night. We should be somewhere I can talk to you on Wednesday at m your time. Listen in then. Much love sweetie.

day was Wednesday and it was four in the afternoon. I listened to the cond message.

eed you to do something - Disconnect the telephone and when the plumber mes don't let him in. Be careful – he may be armed. But he shouldn't start ything and he'll be alone. Maurice will come over when he sees him ming. You can trust Maurice. He won't speak English much, but he derstands perfectly. Tell him what I've told you. He has guns and he'll give u back up if needed; but this bloke is only semi-pro so he should take the t and bugger off easily enough.

ot to go darling. Won't be able to speak on Wednesday after all. I miss you.

as angry as hell. I felt she was playing silly games with me. First of all the ff with the radio - did she think this was a film? - and then the mysterious ff about the plumber. And why would I need an old bloke to support me?

*   *   *   *   *

e plumber turned up with Maurice a day and a half later. Sally was right; he s only semi-pro. He was too well groomed, his shoes looked expensive and an and he babbled unconvincingly about a problem with shared local drains. He said he would need to inspect everywhere there was a water supply and other areas and I told him there were no problems and he had no permission to do anything, so please get lost. He looked from Maurice, who winked at me several times unnecessarily, and me and went, cursing in French.

I watched the 'plumber' go to the edge of the land at the front of Sally's house in one of those stupid but incredibly serviceable tiny Citroën 2CV vans. When he pulled onto the main road a car drew across his path and two blokes got out and bundled him in.

Uncle Tom and a mate at work again, I thought.

Maurice did me the honour of explaining that *Madamoiselle Sarah* had done some of his countrymen a favour recently and some unpleasant element had decided to tap her 'phone and try to cause problems for her. He and his chums would be taken care of. Maurice chuckled and wandered off.

I was shocked that even here, where I thought Sally was safely away from danger, there were threats.

It was pretty much nearly two weeks before she came back. I was angry but immensely relieved. I'd heard nothing since the radio messages, although I'd spent most of each day and half the nights checking. I'd worked myself into a bit of a state but tried to calm down over the past couple of days.

Not a word. Not a single bloody word did Sally tell me about what had happened and she was a bit offish with me. There were bruises on her arms and a nasty cut across her lower back. Nothing. I asked, but she just shrugged.

'Don't tell me you walked into a tree; or did it fall on you this time?'

'I criticised the display in Harrods *Way In* boutique and one of the sales assistants cut up nastily.'

She drank more than I'd seen her do before and I had trouble keeping up. A lot of the time she was silent and when I started to protest she'd say something that made me shut up as if I were doing something that upset her. Then she'd be sweet and tender and wonderful and I'd feel guilty.

It was over a month before she prepared to leave again.

I was forceful. 'I'm coming with you and if you don't let me, I'll follow you.'

'Don't be an idiot. You wouldn't last a day. And if you try to follow me I'll have the guys duff you up and throw you away somewhere.'

'They don't scare me and I don't believe you anyway.'

ou'd be breaking the Official Secrets Act. I'd have Nathalie get you thrown in
ol.'

or God's sake! I just want to ...'

hen do as I ask you. I couldn't bear it if anything happened to you and that
ould keep me off balance. I can't afford that. I know it's hard waiting, but you
ve to. It's the only way this can work. You'll get used to it.'

that what they told you?'

ho?'

ne others.' Ouch. As soon as I had I wished I hadn't said that.

vas water off a duck's back and Sally just said without emotion
nly a few of them. Ta-ra.'

*   *   *   *   *

idn't get easier, of course, and I began to feel like a prisoner. I wandered
ound the big house, took the car and gambled, stayed overnight at what had
come *our* hotel, in *our* suite, drank *our* champagne and played at *our* table.

e waiters and staff that always greeted us with smiles and absolute
vitude only gave me glancing acknowledgement and I missed her even
re.

as lonely as hell. I didn't dare move beyond our little patch of comfort and
ture into, say, Paris, because I was waiting for her to call. She'd said she
uld and I shouldn't bother with the radio again, but of course there never
re any telephone calls. She had clearly decided that it wasn't necessary
ause I had to learn to wait.

I waited.

as good financially. I'd lost a bundle, but made it back and some on top,
gely thanks to Sally having tutored me well. I still had much of what
halie had given me. That offered some distraction when Sally was away.

netimes it was a month, once nearly two, before Sally got the call. But
en she did she went without hesitation, clearly because she chose to go.

several occasions Sally would return with all of the others, for what reason
not sure. Maybe it was for debriefing. Various permutations would go for
ks or tuck themselves away in one of the big reception rooms. Or maybe it
just a celebration of the fact they had all survived.

There was much drinking and everyone seemed fairly happy to be around each other for a day or two, except Alexandra who remained dark and moody and seemed capable of drinking everyone else under the table. She and Sally actually spoke pleasantly to each other on several occasions, although Sally was still rather sarcastic at times.

They seemed so comfortable with each other and I felt like a spare what's it, an uninvited guest at a house party for a small, elite group of guests. Don't get me wrong; they were all, in their own ways, pleasant to me. Nathalie actually made small talk and laughed once or twice. I wondered about her too: she was absolutely gorgeous and when she loosened up was incredibly attractive and charming. I felt quite honoured that she didn't feel the need to treat me with the harsh manner she often displayed. But then again, perhaps it was because they weren't working, or perhaps Sally laid down rules.

Alexandra always looked angry, but she could be warm and considerate for brief periods and asked me a lot about myself one night over a bottle of brandy. I asked her about Russia and she became quite emotional. She told me about some of the beautiful things there and some of the dreadful and then withdrew and went off alone with another bottle.

TM and HH did a lot of drinking. TM often looked tense, but HH had an easy, relaxed manner about him. I'd expected something from TM who I was convinced was keen on Sally, but the only thing I ever got was one warm evening as we drank champagne outside the house. The others were inside.

'I'm only going to say this once' he said without even looking at me. 'If you make her happy, that's fine. Hurt her and I'll kill you.'

'I have no intention of …'

'Behave yourself and remember.' He turned and went inside and never said anything like that again.

Sally drank an awful lot sometimes but not to the point of passing out. And the accent varied, sometimes across very short periods of time, even just minutes, depending on what was being discussed. Sally clearly either chose to do it or perhaps it was that she chose how she would be when alone with me. Either way, I stopped trying to work it out.

They all drank like professionals. Nathalie could put it away at a frightening pace once she got started, and I never once saw Alexandra look even remotely intoxicated despite the amount she threw down her neck.

TM could be moody. He was all right so long as he was listened to. He had a habit, I learned, of delivering little lectures and they could be about anything. He was very knowledgeable. He'd go on about a wine from the cellar, or a car, or the history of Parisian architecture, until in frustration Nathalie told him to shut up. He always dressed and groomed himself immaculately and made fuss about it, but you could tell that underneath there was something else, something serious.

oody rude woman, Nathalie, but gorgeous and I have to say I grew quite nd of her. She had something about her. I learnt quickly that it was she ho'd brought them together. I got the impression she felt responsible for em and Sally told me Nathalie's worst fear was losing one of them.

ey came and went quickly and then Sally and I were mercifully alone again.

t we'd fallen into a routine. Nothing wrong with that, except it did something me. Something sad happened. I began to feel like a pet, locked away in lly's other world while she was on Her Majesty's service. I actually never nt further than between the house, hotel and casino. I had no job except to it until Sally returned and then be with her constantly. I was to ask no estions and wasn't to comfort her about any injury or oddness. She was wn up and tough, she told me, and didn't need to be *molly coddled like a ild*. There was coldness to her, almost as if she was able to just switch off in, emotion or even the weather whenever she wanted.

vas difficult but I realised I was so much in love with her that I couldn't stop.

e worst time was when she'd been away for almost two weeks. When she ne back it was a terrible time. She was covered in bruises and she had a above her left eye which was a ghastly green and mauve. She wouldn't e a doctor but she limped for weeks after and often held her hip and fought ainst the pain. I'd never seen her show any sign of being in pain before so it st have been bad.

ouldn't contain myself and one afternoon as she tried to rest, stretched out a chaise longue on the terrace at the back of the house, I lost it and nanded she tell me what happened.

ly looked desperately anguished but I kept at it and she gave in. I felt en afterwards but I couldn't help it. Sally told me that it had been a stupid g, a small thing that had resulted in all of them nearly being killed. She had nder control, she said. Nathalie and the others were dealing with a mob of rderous Chinese and she was keeping the reinforcements back with efully placed shots. TM was with her and without warning he suddenly nt off to investigate a sound behind them. She took her eyes off the osition to check where he was and a group of men were suddenly on m. There was a fight, she said, and she couldn't get to her weapons ckly enough and had to - she said *Get physical* and I shuddered at the ught of what had happened. She said Alexandra and HH had clocked what s happening and provided a distraction so that Sally could do some oting and that was the end of it. TM had taken a bad hammering and she d she got off lightly.

I asked why they hadn't been shot and Sally said it was because the men the
were up against enjoyed hurting people too much to miss an opportunity. The
thought of Sally being involved with such horror was too much and I exploded
angry with her, yes, for getting herself into such a filthy business; but I was
also torn to pieces by the knowledge that she would do it all over again if
Nathalie Endeavour asked her. I think I actually shed tears but I stopped when
Sally got up and limped away without a word.

We didn't really speak for several days and I slept on a sofa downstairs for
three nights. Each morning I would wake and Sally would be lying on the
carpet next to me. When I spoke she'd simply roll over and leave me.

I tried to apologise but she wouldn't have it. I tried to get her to see a doctor
and she told me that her physical health was her business alone and I should
never try to interfere.

There was an uneasy silence between us and I drank too much.

One afternoon, when I'd pretty much decided we'd had it and I should sober
up and leave, she walked calmly past me and said she was going for a ride
and would see me later.

I'd positioned myself in the hall and from where I sat on the floor, propped up
against a great Italian credenza with a bottle of whisky, I could see anyone
who came into the house from the front or the back. There were only the two
entrances.

I had no idea how she'd got into the house without my seeing her, but then
again, she is Sally Twitchett. I was suddenly aware of the click of heels on th
staircase above me. I looked up and there was Sally, paused on the staircas
and looking absolutely magnificent. The bruises had gone and she wore full
make up and a tiny lime green chiffon thing. She looked as if she were about
to be photographed for Vogue. Sally didn't say a word, but came and knelt
beside me and that was it. I sobered up immediately and knew I wasn't going
anywhere.

Later, she told me that I had to understand. She said that I could never be
with her when she was working because she would be too worried about me
and that would be too much of a distraction. She used TM as an example. H
was fine, she said, so long as he did as he was told, so that she didn't have
worry. She said they all knew the same and relied on each other not to put t
others at risk. It was instinct, she said, and couldn't be taught.

When I asked her about TM and if it was work that kept them from each oth
she told me that if they were lovers she would be so distracted by the fear
he'd be hurt she wouldn't be able to do the job and that she couldn't stop it.
'It's what I have to do' she said. About TM she added 'He's a brother; a
brother in arms, but not mine. That's reserved for you.'

pleaded with Sally to give it up. She told me she couldn't. She said there
were so many awful people and such bad things in the world that somebody
had to deal with them, to protect decent people. She told me there weren't
that many who could do it. I asked her why she had to be one of them and
she said she believed that she had been given something special, something
that would keep her safe and help her do what needed to be done.

When I tried to argue with her Sally fell silent and struggled with something.
Then she told me that she believed she was who she was and could do what
she did because of her past. She told me what happened to her family, when
she was six years old. Her father worked for the Foreign Office and had
discovered a plot to overthrow the government of the little South American
state he was posted to. The people responsible found out and bombed the
family's house. Sally had been planting flowers with the girl her mother had
hired as a nanny-cum-maid because the girl, from London's East End, had
been down on her luck. Sally and the maid survived but Sally's parents and
baby brother were killed. This, Sally told me, was why she had been given her
gifts, so that she could help prevent others suffering the way she and her
family had.

Every time Sally helped Nathalie Endeavour rid the world of some horrible
threat and prevent innocent people being killed, she somehow counter-
balanced what had happened to her family.

Got it. I understood.

But it didn't make it any easier the next time she left.

*   *   *   *   *

I waited three weeks without a word.

Sally had promised me that she would do everything she could to keep in
touch when she was away. She would telephone, she would write, she said,
and joked about sending postcards so that I could start a collection that would
chart her travels with Nathalie Endeavour.

There came to be an understanding between us and although I couldn't ever
accept the dreadful risks she took, I knew I couldn't stop her and that any
attempt to do so would ruin what we had forever.

Sally really did try to reassure me that she could keep herself safe. She even
tried to teach me martial arts and threw me all over the house and grounds as
if I were a rag doll. I became so angry one day I really did try to hit her but I
didn't stand a chance and she just put me down and giggled, half tipsy on
champagne.

But it didn't help and when she didn't contact me I became hopelessly worried
and angry.

Then there were more postcards: one from Rome, another from Tokyo. There were no codes on these, no veiled messages.

All ok.

Bored.

Done Rome too many times.

S XX

Japan is strange but beautiful.

Not much chance to see anything of interest.

Try not to worry.

S XXX

Try not to worry! Bloody cheek!

Italy and Japan. I got drunk and ran through possible scenarios. Whatever she was involved in it had to be big - international. Perhaps she was tracking someone she had to kill. Perhaps she was running from someone. Maybe she'd been hurt and didn't want to say. Or perhaps one of the others had been hurt and she was waiting to find out if they'd make it.

I even wondered if perhaps I was just one of several blokes she had stowed away. For all I knew she had other places to hide them. This idea festered until I became convinced it had to be true. It was easier, of course, than wondering if she was hurt or worse and anyway, how could the most beautiful and exciting girl in the world not have her choice of men wherever she was?

I'd always told myself that if something appeared too good to be true it was and I applied this to my relationship with Sally and drove myself crazy.

I was off. I didn't mean it to be permanent but I felt stifled, censored, tormented and I was angry as hell. I told Maurice I was going away for a while but that I would be back. No, I didn't have a forwarding address or telephone number, but I was probably going to Paris. He raised his eyebrows and I strongly suspected he knew something I didn't. In fact, that was exactly the case.

It occurred to me that I might be just one more in a string of men Sally had entertained at her home in France and I wondered how many Maurice had met. I concluded it would probably be all of them. It would account for his overtly protective behaviour towards Sally.

fetched up in Paris and drank and brooded about Sally Twitchett, completely unaware that she had an apartment on the Île Saint-Louis and was actually frequenting it at that very time. She and the others had returned from Japan and were mopping up something or other; I never found out what. She hadn't told me about the Paris apartment. She hadn't told me a lot of things.

I sat in a bar one night and drank far too much. I was engaged in conversation with another English bloke who was fed up with women and we drowned our sorrows together.

'What's yours like?' he asked me in all innocence. I wished I could have told him the truth.

She works freelance for this secret service dolly bird who also runs a boutique in her spare time, you know, when she's not fighting and killing people who pose a risk to the free and innocent. She's absolutely stunning, but mine is the most beautiful girl in the world. Blonde. An impossible blonde goddess. She risks her life a hundred times a year and kills when she has to. She's a magician with a gun. Never misses. She's an absolute dream, in every sense of the word. Loaded. Dresses like a fashion model. Drives like Graham Hill and Stirling Moss put together. She can break your heart with a simple smile. Keeps me a virtual prisoner when she's at home. Quite possibly schizophrenic or at least very troubled, but who cares? Instead I told him: 'Blonde. Absolute stunner. Loaded. Talented. Dresses like a model.'

'Sounds fantastic! You lucky bastard!'

'Keeps me locked away sometimes.'

'Kinky too, eh? You're even more of a …'

'No. Not like that. She leaves me for weeks on end with no word of explanation. I hang around waiting for her to contact me.'

'Ah. Bad luck. Still, compensations, eh?'

I regarded him with distaste, then dismissed him.

'You don't understand.'

'They're all the same mate. Mine's a right tart. Bit of a dolly bird like yours, but

'She's no dolly bird!' I thundered and was asked to leave the bar.

In another bar I decided that I was treated almost like a mascot by Sally's bunch. That's why they're so open around me, as if I don't really count. They take me for granted, all of them, and treat me like some mascot, or pet. *Sally's pet.* That's what I'll call myself, I thought. I was drunk in Paris with a small fortune, had the most beautiful girl in the world for company when she was at home, and I was miserable as sin. I was feeling pretty bad that night.

Any night like that brings its own compensations the next morning. In my experience you either feel so lousy you don't remember how bad you felt the night before, or you wake up and everything's suddenly, instantly better. This morning was different. I didn't feel bad physically but nothing looked or felt any better.

It would end, I told myself, one of several ways. Either Sally would grow tired of me or I of the agony of waiting for her to return. Or she would be killed. If that happened, I knew one of the others would let me know. If it were TM ... no, it wouldn't be him. He'd be too upset. Maybe HH. *Look, I'm sorry old man ... I have bad news. It's about Sally ...* Or it would be Nathalie; direct, then angry because she'd let Sally get killed and then she would be very, very upset. Alexandra would be very emotional, I decided. But she wouldn't telephone. She would come in person. We would cry together, I decided. I've never seen her do it, but I'm sure she can cry. Or maybe they'd all buy it and I'd never find out. Sally would simply never come back and I'd never hear a thing.

How could I live like that? Just waiting to hear she was dead? Hanging around every day, too worried and angry to get on with anything else in life except drinking and gambling. Even I hadn't imagined such a life for myself.

Ah, but when Sally came back. When she looked at me, and held me ...

I kept a photograph of Sally with me whenever I left the house. It shows Sally on d'Artagnan, dressed in one of my white shirts and nothing else, hair flying in the sun. I'd taken it a couple of months before and when I collected the prints the little French guy who'd developed the film spent a long time admiring it. He asked if she was a model or an actress and when I said neither he said I should send the picture to a fashion magazine, or enter a competition.

I brooded over the photograph for hours. Sally was magnificent. She was never happier than when she was with the old horse and her face was angelic bliss. Just a look from Sally could break me apart and I'd do absolutely anything for her. That was worth the price, wasn't it? I didn't even know that for sure anymore.

*　　*　　*　　*　　*

When I got back I was still feeling lousy, but I had at least resolved to be good and bide my time. I would talk to Sally about our future when she returned. course, I had no intention of ending the relationship; I couldn't. I knew that I would have to go through a lot more agony before I got to the stage of even considering it. No, there were things that could be done, I was convinced of at, and we could move on. Perhaps she'd even consider giving it up if I proposed marriage. I was prepared to go all in.

wanted to get back as quickly as I could after I realised what a twit I'd been nd wasn't prepared for what was waiting when I turned down the road that d to Sally's place.

athalie's yellow E-Type Jaguar was parked on the drive, as was TM's Alvis.

ney like their cars and whenever possible they'll take them with them, rtainly if there's an air or ferry service they can use. Alexandra is the ception and regards her green Porsche (green for goodness' sake!) as a ol. TM is in love with his Alvis TD51. The big bloke, HH opts for a very ately but powerful midnight blue Jaguar Mk 10. Of course, Sally has a little et. In London, a white Mercedes 230SL and a white Marcus 1600GT for ckup; in France it's the white Mistral Spyder but she'd taken it with her so I as using the little white BMW. I asked Sally once why all her cars were ite and she told me *It's the only way of telling if they're clean, silly!*

hen I saw the two cars several things hit me at once and I felt sick. Either mething had happened to Sally - her Maserati wasn't on the drive - and ey'd come to tell me, or she was using them for support to kick me out. ually bad was my concern that if she had returned, Sally would have found e gone. True, Maurice may have told her I'd gone to Paris for a while, but I ew she'd be angry and if she hadn't yet seen him …

e big double entrance doors were open - it was a warm day – and as I went to them I heard two female voices behind a closed door. I couldn't make t what was being said but one of the women wasn't happy and I realised it s Nathalie's voice.

exandra leaned against a wall dressed in her usual gypsy-style black skirt d shirt. She was frowning and said 'So - you are back.'

hat's going on?' I asked and started towards the study. I could hear thalie thundering on and she was clearly in there with Sally.

ey fight' Alexandra said 'and you will leave.' She wandered off towards one he reception rooms and without knowing why I followed her. I didn't see er of the blokes around.

hat do you mean they're fighting?' I asked.

ey make argument' Alexandra said and filled two glasses with red gundy.

hat about?' I asked although I wasn't really interested. I wanted them gone hat I could be with Sally.

'Sally leaves to come here. Because you are gone.'

'Didn't the old man tell her where I was?' I was really worried.

'Who is of knowing?' Alexandra shrugged and I suddenly felt that she was playing with me. She sat and sipped wine and just stared at me.

'Look' I said 'I don't know what's going on or why you're always fetching up here, but …'

'Is worried. For you!' Alexandra tossed her head and was suddenly standing with a face like thunder. 'Why you leave no note for Sally?'

'Why the hell should I? She takes off for God knows where without a word for weeks!'

I was really angry that Alexandra was poking her nose into mine and Sally's business and said so.

'Pah!' Alexandra exploded and tossed her head again, fighting the hair back from her face. 'Zatknis!'

'I don't speak Russian.'

'I say *"Shut up!"*'

'Thanks. You saying they're arguing about me?' I sat down.

'Some! And of other things! Big things.'

'Well, I'm fed up with all this crap. It they're arguing about me I've a right to know what they're saying.' I got up to go but Alexandra stood in my way.

I couldn't believe that Alexandra would physically prevent me from going to Sally in her house and said so. Alexandra told me that if she needed to she would and the look on her face told me to believe her.

I was contemplating how having a serious run in with Alexandra would turn out when the door to the study burst open and Nathalie thundered out yelling 'You're a bloody impossible woman!'

When Nathalie walked in and saw me her face was thunder.

I said hi and started to go to Sally but Nathalie walked up to me and slapped me around the left side of my face. She did something and put all her weight behind the slap and I went down.

'You bloody moron!'

s I picked myself and my dignity off the floor, Nathalie poured wine and ank, then poured more.

/hat the hell was that for?' I asked.

he's been worried because of you, and that means she wasn't properly on e job!!' Nathalie sounded even fiercer than Alexandra.

ooked at Sally as she walked slowly into the room. 'She thinks I should op.' Sally sat on a chair and made it look like a throne. 'How have you en?' She seemed very detached and I knew something serious was going .

reat! Until about two minutes ago. What the hell's going on?'

do wish you wouldn't shout' Sally said quietly 'it really doesn't suit you.'

exandra muttered something I couldn't get and left the room, closing the or behind her.

aited for one of them to say something. When they didn't I said 'If it's not o much trouble, Nathalie, I'd like to be alone with Sally.'

athalie looked ready to hit me again as she said 'Not until I've had my say!'

ou really have caused a bit of a problem, darling' Sally said as if she were king to a sales assistant.

op talking in riddles and tell me what's going on!' I was shouting again and lly made a disapproving noise and poured herself a huge gin and tonic.

ow did you know we were in Paris?' Nathalie demanded.

idn't.'

on't lie to me!' Now Nathalie was shouting.

lly said 'For God's sake! All right - here it is. We were in Paris. We were shing the job. Then you turn up.'

of a bloody coincidence wasn't it?' Nathalie demanded.

ad no idea you were in Paris! I got a bloody postcard! From Japan!'

ent you one from Rome too' Sally said as if she was in some way offended.

ey arrived on the same day' I said, because they had, although the dates e nearly a week apart.

'Well, I can hardly be held responsible for the shortcomings of the postal services' Sally said, pouring more gin and tonic.

'Never mind the bloody postcards!' Nathalie exploded. 'Tell me how you knew we were in Paris!'

'I didn't. I wasn't even sure I was going there myself. I just wound up there. I wanted some … space. How did you know anyway?'

'Maurice told me' Sally said 'but TM saw you well before I spoke to him.'

'Saw me?' I must have sounded like a twit.

'Yes' Sally said and this time she sounded upset. 'He tried to get to you to speak but the opposition had made him and he didn't want to put you at risk. By the time he'd dealt with them you'd disappeared.'

'The point is' began Nathalie, and this time she wasn't shouting 'from that moment on Sally knew you were in Paris. If you'd seen and acknowledged any of us and the opposition saw, you'd have been a target for them as much as us.'

'Some rather bad people followed us back from Japan' Sally said in a matter of fact way 'and they would have enjoyed chopping you up for sport.'

'Listen to me' Nathalie said to me urgently. 'She wasn't able to focus on the job. She nearly got herself killed …'

'Oh, now that wasn't really the case, was it?' Sally said and actually giggled

'If she's with me I need her full commitment. How can she do that when you're off walkabout doing whatever bloody stupid thing you were doing?'

'I didn't know where you were' Sally said. 'We tried to track you down but you just disappeared and I …' She let the sentence die and suddenly looked up again.

'Now do you get it?' Nathalie demanded.

I did get it. So far as Sally was concerned I could have been bumped off, captured, or maybe she thought I'd had enough and left her.

'We didn't know where to look' Nathalie said angrily 'or what the bloody hell you were playing at!'

Sally was quite calm again and I didn't like the way she just sat there and let Nathalie do her thing.

What the hell does it have to do with you anyway? From my understanding
he's not …'

don't want to lose anyone.' Nathalie was in a short blue dress with white
polka dots. She looked stunning but a very seasoned and very angry
professional dealer in bad things. 'And if she's distracted and worried then
she's at risk. And that means we all are. '

Sally wasn't arguing and just sat there.

She thought you might have come back. For all we knew you'd been made
and followed. That's why we all came, you bloody idiot!'

I stuttered a bit and eventually managed to say that it was pure coincidence
they were in Paris, that I'd had no idea they were and that I hadn't seen any of
them. The chances of my crossing the paths of Nathalie and her lot twice by
accident must have been astronomical, but I'd managed it and was feeling
stupid.

Nathalie thinks I should stop.' Sally said it in a matter of fact way as if she
were choosing a carpet colour.

Stop what?'

Either my relationship with you or working with her.'

She should have been upset. I remember thinking that at the time. She was
so detached.

s for you two to work it out.' Nathalie drained her glass of wine and put it
down. 'But I want you to understand what's at stake here. It's not a game.
Work it out.'

I don't know if Nathalie was talking to me, Sally or both of us but she left
without another word and actually closed the door after her.

Sally looked at me and said 'She's right. The two don't mix.'

at and rubbed my face, which stung like hell.

said I was sorry and explained that I'd got bored or some such nonsense.

o. I think you got angry.' Sally was much too calm and I feared the worst.

Well, wouldn't you be?' I got angry. You expect me to stay cooped up here
waiting for you to come back? I'm worried sick about you every day and night
when you're away. Why couldn't you bloody well telephone? And what was
that silly game with the radio, anyway? Why did you do that and never use it
again?'

'Because I couldn't! And using the radio was wrong. There are ways to track signals. It could have brought bad things here.'

'I didn't mean to worry you. But I'm not convinced you couldn't find a minute to call.'

Sally put her head in her hands. 'I can't! I can't take my mind off the job and to speak with you I'd have to do that! I'd have to come out of my world and into ours. And you'd ask too many questions, and I can't do it …!'

I understood. To do what she did she couldn't be my Sarah and had to be her own Sally Twitchett.

I apologised again.

'You wanted me to know what it feels like.'

'It wasn't like that …'

I looked at her huge hazel eyes and wanted to hug her. I moved to do so and she let me, but didn't respond.

'Yes you did. You wanted me to know what it feels like to be worried sick about someone who's missing.'

'Well, maybe I did; just a little bit.'

'But I already did know. I've known it for a long time, you see. I've been taught the lesson several times over. And I don't want to go through it again. I can't.'

I looked at her and my heart tore as I realised what a beautiful but tormented creature she really was and the pain she'd gone through.

'I'm really sorry. I …'

'I need to work it out. I don't want to lose you … but I don't know if I can cope with the worry.'

'I can handle myself …' I knelt beside her and held her hand, which was soft as a child's but cold.

'Yes. To a degree. But that man who came … I played it down, but …'

'He looked like a pushover. What was all that about anyway? Maurice said something about you having done someone a favour …'

'It's complicated and boring. Very boring.'

'People coming to your house with guns is boring?'

Yes. That's the whole point.'

Tell me the point Sally. I've been thinking a lot and I really need to…'

Sally got up and poured wine for both of us. 'I know you've been thinking. I know it was wrong of me to expect you to wait, not knowing … well, how I was.'

Exactly! Let me go with you. I'm pretty good with a gun. You've seen I can shoot. It isn't that long ago I did my National Service. We can keep an eye on each other. Even if I stay in the background at least we'll both be able to …'

Oh, you poor, silly man!' There was pity and anguish in her voice and I didn't like it.

I said it would be better than her going off and leaving me. Sally looked genuinely upset and I thought she was going to cry.

No. It's not. I told you before: you wouldn't last a day.'

Look here, Sally …' I wasn't going to lose this round. I couldn't.

Don't. Please don't. It doesn't matter whether you can shoot well or fight. That's not what it's about …' She touched my cheek and smiled, but it wasn't a smile of happiness. 'You just don't have what's necessary. In here.' She tapped her heart. 'You're too nice.'

I can do what's necessary when needed. You know that. I would have shot that bloke in the chateau in Switzerland!'

Yes. You might have. But you didn't. You'll always hesitate. I can't. And I don't, unless I'm distracted. Don't you get it?'

So: if I'm with you we'll probably both get killed, and if I don't stay here like a good little boy you'll worry and probably get killed anyway, or someone else will!'

That's pretty much it. Please understand. My business doesn't allow for … relationships. I could no more take you with me than a soldier could take his wife into battle. The people we deal with are brutal, vicious, even crazy killers. When we have to kill it's to protect innocent people or ourselves and there's no room for hesitation. But when we're in the thick of it I don't think like that… none of us can. We just have to react. And you don't have that instinct. You're so … you're too nice.'

We'd finished our wine and collected the decanter of whisky from the console by the window. I looked out and saw the two blokes on the terrace outside. Nathalie and Alexandra were sitting at a table in a shaded grassy area, deep in conversation. Sally's own little private security detail.

I sat next to her and fought the need to take her in my arms and kiss her. It wasn't easy. I asked if she would consider giving up working with Nathalie, but already had the answer.

Sally sighed and drank. 'I don't know. I don't know if I could. You see, she's .. important. They all are. To me, I mean.'

'And I'm not?'

'It's not the same. They … they need me. They need what I can do.'

'And you need them. Or what they do.'

Sally stared into her glass. 'Yes … yes, I do. At least I think I do …' She looked up at me and she was suddenly tormented and vulnerable and I was desperate to show her a way out.

'You could, you know …' I took both of her hands in mine. 'There might be something that could help.'

She started to cry. 'I can't … I can't imagine what …'

'Let me love you. Stop fighting it and let me love you. Nathalie will cope …'

Sally let out a sob and tears fell onto her tiny dress. 'I don't know what I'd become …'

That made sense to me. I'd tried to overlook the two Sallys I'd experienced. I suppose I'd been pretty lucky to have had so much of one. But the other was as much her and in a way maybe even more important.

'So … what are you going to decide? Or have you already?'

'No. It's difficult. Can't you see …?'

I went for it. 'Give it up. Even if it's only to see how we get on. If we can't make a go of it you can go back …'

'Please don't make me …'

The look on her face was breaking my heart but I pushed on. ' I knew I couldn't carry on the way we'd been and said 'You can't have it both ways. You can't, Sally. You have to make a decision.'

'I know. That's what Alexandra told me.'

I was shocked that Sally would have discussed such a personal thing with the Russian, but then again I was getting used to being shocked and realised I didn't really know very much at all about the other life Sally lived.

said I was surprised.

Alexandra's not stupid. She knows what's been happening to us. And she knows what it's like … to be alone and to want someone. To have no family, and then to … be a part of something, even 'though it puts your life at risk, that seems to make it worthwhile, at least for a little while.'

Are you telling me you go out risking your life because you need Nathalie's lot and it makes your life worth living?'

Not quite. And that's not exactly what I said. It's much more complicated than that. But I have to keep doing it … at least for a while. I can't change that.'

Well, I can't stay here a virtual prisoner while you do it.'

Sally took her hands from mine and examined them as if she expected to see something nasty; or perhaps it was for signs of all the times she'd used them to kill.

We could have a good life together, you and I. And you know I love you.'

Sally stopped looking at her hands but didn't look at me. 'Yes. Yes, I know you do. And I love you too… in my own way.'

I wondered what the hell *In my own way* meant.

Sally looked at me again and this time I didn't recognise the look on her face at all. 'I'm not a normal girl, am I? You can't expect me to be able to put everything aside and focus entirely on my feelings for you.'

I didn't ask you to. Look; get rid of this lot and let's spend time together. Whatever you decide … well, I'll go along with it.'

I don't want you to say that.'

Why?'

Because you won't be able to. You can't come with me and I can't stop going. And you won't be able to stand staying alone and safe. And I won't be able to stand worrying about you. Damn you bloody people!'

She shot up, stormed across the room, went through the door and ran up the stairs.

I drank two more very large whiskies and wondered what the hell I should do. It was seven thirty in the evening.

I pushed Sally and she'd made it clear what she thought. I couldn't see a way forward to give us both what we wanted. It was really quite simple: to love

Sally Twitchett I had to do exactly what she wanted. This meant her leading a double life. There would be weeks, months maybe, of wonderful times for us together, injuries notwithstanding, and days, weeks even, of agonising loneliness and worry while she did what she clearly had to go on doing. I would have to be a good boy and be there when she returned and not ask why she was limping, or had a black eye or cuts in odd places. There would always be a silver plated Colt automatic under her pillow and if she didn't feel like talking for three days straight, so be it.

But it would be worth it. I made that decision after another couple of large whiskies and prepared to go to her. To hell with it! I told myself. I'd give in. She'd win. That wasn't such a price to pay for keeping Sally.

Before I reached the door it opened. Alexandra walked quickly in and leant against it as it closed.

I was drunk enough not to be intimidated and said 'Now what?'

'You have decided to go to her?' Alexandra wasn't budging so I sat down again.

'Yes. She wins.'

'Maybe you are not big idiot after all.' She helped herself to whisky.

I got up and headed for the door again.

'She rides horse' Alexandra said casually and poured more whisky.

Until Alexandra had closed it minutes ago the door had been open and I hadn't seen Sally come down the stairs. I said so.

Alexandra stared at me and said again 'She rides horse.'

I went to the stairs and then up to Sally's room - our room, as it had become Sally wasn't there. There was a bathroom and dressing room and I checked them. The little dress Sally had been wearing was on the floor of the dressing room but that told me little. Then something odd happened. From behind rail of Sally's outrageously expensive clothes Alexandra appeared.

I got it straight away but Alexandra showed me the little door anyway. 'Is for plan of escape' she said unnecessarily. I went through and down the stairs and very quickly I was opening a panel in the dining room wall. From there Sally could have gone to the kitchen and out, which is obviously what she'd done. I told Alexandra that I'd never known about it before but she didn't say anything and poured herself something from a decanter. I joined her and found out it contained brandy. I hadn't noticed it before then remembered we never used the dining room at all.

ecause I felt it appropriate to say something and was angry I said 'Seems
ou know Sally better than I do.'

lexandra scoffed and arranged herself on a console. She looked fantastic
nd wore what I thought might have been a mischievous expression on her
ce. She folded her arms and said 'If anyone knows of Sally, it is Nathalie.
ut who knows? There is only of what she gives to know. And that is … poof!'
ne made a frustrated gesture with one hand.

o how long have Sally and Nathalie known each other?' I asked.

ears. For how much, you should ask of them.'

id they know each other before you arrived?'

f course!' Alexandra seemed annoyed that I had to ask such a question.
ally is first of us.'

see.' I didn't really, but at least I knew more than I had to date. I'd asked
ally several times about how Nathalie had gathered her little team around
r and she just laughed and said she couldn't remember it all and anyway it
eemed like forever so what did it matter?

r some reason it mattered to me.

nis annoys?'

did.

ally is much to give annoyance.' She poured more brandy for herself and
ust the decanter at me. I agreed with her.

en Alexandra surprised me again. 'But for all, she is good woman.'

ld Alexandra she surprised me.

ne has of good heart. And she will protect all of us. This we know.'

e irritates you' I said. 'I thought you couldn't stand each other.'

e has of much stupidness!' Alexandra launched herself off the console and
ced, waving her right hand in the air as she did so. 'Always she makes of
pid sayings! Always she talks of clothes!'

what reason I'm not sure but I told Alexandra that Sally had been quite
erent here with me. This didn't surprise her.

course! Here there is another piece of her! Somebody else to be.'

I wasn't sure quite what Alexandra was getting at but I said 'I think they're all part of Sally. What I'm not sure about is which one is strongest.'

At this Alexandra blazed at me. 'Fool! All are of same! How you do not see this?'

I told her I wasn't convinced and that I really believed the Sally, or Sarah I had experienced was the stronger side of her and that she only used the silly London dolly bird stuff when she got anxious about the job.

Alexandra spoke to me like a stupid school boy and told me that Sally never got anxious about the job. True, she said, she could be annoying and inappropriate and why the ridiculous clothes? But she said she'd realised that all of these parts made up the whole and one couldn't be separated from the other. To try to do so, she cautioned me, was heading for big trouble.

'If you make of her to be one part, to be with you, the other will fight. And of same way before.'

'The other way round' I corrected her. It made sense. But it meant there would be no way I could win. Although I'd decided to give up fighting, I really had believed that with time I could win Sally over. Now it didn't seem such a possibility.

'You thought you could make of her another woman? One side only, to be for you?'

I just looked at her.

'Men! Always you think this is possible.'

I protested but it didn't make any difference. Then I said that none of us are just one person and that we often choose who we want to be when we're with other people.

'You think this possible when gun at head? You are stupid boy.'

The more she said the worse I felt. She was telling me I'd been naïve, thinking that I could choose the part of Sally that I wanted and make her lose the rest. I told her so and said why didn't she just say it?

'Is said.'

Then Nathalie walked in. 'What're you two up to?' She went straight for the brandy decanter and I thought again how at home everybody made themselves in Sally's house; but it went along with the idea that they were so tight with each other they didn't need to be anything else.

Nathalie downed the brandy in one and refilled and demanded of me 'Well?'

'Alexandra' I began 'has been giving me a psychology lesson and pointed out that Sally has multiple facets to her character and I was stupid to think that I could try to make her be just the one I wanted.'

'Glad to see you're not slipping' Nathalie said to Alexandra and then to me 'She's very good at weighing people up, you see.'

I said I'd noticed and added 'Perhaps I'll ask her opinion of you sometime.'

Alexandra said 'Is simple. She makes life to do good. For *Her Majesty* and old England.' There was more than a hint of sarcasm in the Russian's voice but Nathalie just poured more brandy.

'She makes good job in world of men' Alexandra continued. 'In Russia women are expected to do this but here - pah! Is country for little housewives and men who need them to make cake and garden!'

'Not all men are like that' I said. 'There's a lot of change going on. We're not living in the fifties anymore and …'

'Makes no difference!' Alexandra exclaimed with another dramatic hand gesture. 'Fifties, sixties - all will be the same.'

'I'm not sure that's going to be true' Nathalie said. 'There are the hemlines for one thing …'

'Now you make fun, like Sally!'

'She's not back yet' Nathalie said, ignoring Alexandra's comment and looked at her watch. I went to the window and drew back the wooden blinds that were closed. Outside it was dark although there was a bright moon.

'She can't still be riding' I said urgently.

'There's a moon' Nathalie said 'so of course she can.'

'I've never known her do that before' I said and realised why the two women just looked at me the way they did. They clearly believed I hadn't seen much of the real Sally's behaviour and I was beginning to think they were right.

'Maybe' Alexandra said as she pulled another bottle of brandy from the console 'she does not come back at all.'

'We didn't speak' Nathalie said as she checked her watch again and poured more brandy 'but the impression I got was that your discussion didn't end well.'

'It wasn't a discussion' I said angrily. 'I just tried to … why am I telling you this? It's our business, not yours and …'

'No!' Nathalie slammed her glass down on antique wood. 'It is bloody well my business! You're trying to make her do something she can't … she just can't, do you understand? And it could get her killed! Don't you understand that?'

I could tell Nathalie really did want me to understand. She was drunk and I wondered if this made her more reasonable or more difficult.

'I get it' I said 'but I still say it's not your business. Sally and I must decide for ourselves. It's our future! It's not fair if you try to influence her.'

'I will do what is right!' Nathalie stepped towards me and put hands on hips.

I'd had enough. I turned and headed for the door; but Alexandra put herself against it and looked menacing.

'I'm sure you noticed' Nathalie started and I could tell she was getting up a real head of steam 'the injuries she came back with? Well, you can give yourself a slap on the back for those! All of them! Sally never gets injured unless she's distracted and you, sonny boy, ever since bloody Switzerland, have been a distraction!'

'I didn't ask for it!' I snapped.

'You may not have asked for it, but you haven't had the brains to see what's happening! She's who she is and for that reason she has to do what she does. She could no longer stop than you could be alive and stop breathing! I've had to give her an ultimatum. Either she stops working with me, which she won't, or she finds some way to deal with her relationship with you and still stay focussed on the job. That's trying to keep her alive, not interfering with her future, or yours for that matter!'

Alexandra pushed herself off the door. This time she didn't pour more drink and wandered to the window. 'You have of no idea' she started, shaking her head. I thought I heard genuine sadness in her voice. 'For us …' and she looked at Nathalie who turned away immediately and busied herself with mo drink. '… people like us …' She turned to me and looked at me as if she we struggling for the words ' … we have of anger!' She made a fist. 'We have o need … to make things good … for this … for this we must be alone! Is not us comfort of love …'

'So you disagree with Nathalie?' I asked. 'You think that even if I do as Sally asks and stay here like a good little boy until she gets back, we can't have love?'

Alexandra turned to the window again. 'Pah! For Sally … who has of idea? Perhaps for her, is different.'

I said that was a good point and that they should both remember that.

athalie said I shouldn't get my hopes up. Then she said that if Sally told her
e'd found a way she'd give her a chance.

hen HH came in and I knew by the expression on his face something was
ery wrong.

ust had a word with the old chap' HH said quietly. I knew he meant Maurice.
e's very worried about Sally. Said she knocked him up and asked him to
ok after the horse and then she took off on the motorcycle she keeps at the
ables. Said she was very upset. First time he's ever seen her cry. No
ggage, not even a bag.'

*   *   *   *   *

ey had all been drinking, some more than others, but that didn't deter them.
M was absolutely without pause and immediately said he was driving to
aris to check Sally's apartment there.

H got on the 'phone, utterly convinced he could organise a charter flight to
t them back to London in case that's where Sally was headed. Nathalie said
ey could check out whether Sally had ordered up a flight and got him to do
at first.

athalie made a call to what was clearly some intelligence station and
exandra watched as Nathalie conducted the conversation. My French isn't
lliant but I got the gist of what she was saying. Sally was both at risk and a
k herself. There were people who knew she was associated with Nathalie
d therefore the Secret Service. They didn't know whether anyone was
tching the house. They didn't know what state of mind Sally might be in. If
en, she might prove a security risk.

emanded to know what the hell was going on and said that Sally had the
ht to decide what she did. I was told clearly by Nathalie that I was right, but
t they had protocols in place to protect them and Sally had breached all of
m. It became clear that what TM had told me at Gstaad airport that day
s right: they were never off duty. Each knew where the others were most of
time and nobody went off when they were together without letting the
ers know.

en I asked what I should do, Nathalie told me I should keep out of the
ody way.

*   *   *   *   *

ht passed quickly. There was no sign of Sally and no word from her. TM
ed from Paris to say Sally wasn't there and it didn't look as if she'd been to
flat. I wondered how he'd got in but then told myself of course he'd have a
or just broke in.

HH checked everywhere it might have been possible to charter an aircraft, with no luck.

Alexandra took it upon herself to drive around the area. This meant she was gone all night and when she returned Nathalie quizzed her on where she'd been. Pretty much everywhere that Sally might have reached was the answer.

I asked if they thought it was possible to find Sally if she'd decided to take herself off and didn't want to be found and their looks told me no. I was also told she hadn't ever done this before, although TM told me Sally had on several occasions before *thrown a wobbler* and said she'd had enough, but never during a mission or when there was suspected danger, and she always called one of them to say where she was.

At some point fairly on I'd suggested I check out the hotel and casino we used but TM told me he'd already checked. I started to ask how he knew we used it but stopped because again I realised there probably wasn't very much they didn't know about Sally, and me. I later started to leave to go to the hotel and wait in case Sally showed up but TM stopped me and assured me that 'his contact' would call if she appeared.

It really struck home just how tight this lot were. Even Alexandra seemed to have an almost intimate knowledge of Sally's life. I felt like the only single bloke at a wedding, totally spare and completely useless. It wasn't really surprising: they had to be able to anticipate each other's moves in order to protect themselves. That was why Sally taking off without a word was so worrying.

Nathalie exercised herself much on the telephone, in French and English. She wasn't happy and raised her voice a number of times. I knew what she was doing. She wanted her people to keep a lookout for Sally without making it sound as if she'd gone off half-crazy, which I began to think was the case.

I asked myself several very important questions because nobody really wanted to speak to me. For example, if Sally phoned and learned I was still around, would that deter her from returning? Would it be better if I left? But then again, what would that tell her if she called or came back and I was gone? What would she expect me to do? I really struggled with that one. I'd pretty much decided on the answer when Alexandra walked into the room I was drinking in and draped herself over a big oak chair.

I picked up a glass and offered Alexandra a drink. She just nodded curtly and toyed with her hair. She took the drink and didn't seem to think there was anything to say.

It struck me that all three of these women - Sally, Alexandra and Nathalie - were, as far as I knew, very similar in circumstance. They were all single, had no family and tried to keep personal relationships to the minimum. That was where Sally had gone wrong. And I had to admit that in her world it *was* wrong.

athalie was right. And we'd let it go too far. *I'd* let it go too far. Before Sally
I never had anything even approaching a long-term relationship, certainly
never more than a couple of months. And Sally had told me she'd been hurt
before through letting herself get involved. This made it worse because it had
 mean that for both of us to have indulged ourselves there had to be
something really special between us.

'You wonder what she is to be doing' Alexandra said as she finished her drink
and held the glass out for me to refill. 'You wonder what she wants of you to
do.'

'As Nathalie said - you're very perceptive.'

'From you, there is nothing.' She said it as if it meant nothing and started
drinking again.

'I don't believe that. She'll either want me gone or here when she comes back.
I just can't decide which.'

'Is of no difference.'

'What?'

'Makes no difference. Leave, and she can find if she wants to. If you go,
maybe is for best. Stay, maybe she makes decision. You go, or she quits.'

'Somehow I don't think either option will make her happy.'

'Happy! You are fool!' She shot up from the chair and glared in my face. 'You
are spoilt child! Is nothing for happiness!' She turned, threw a hand in the air,
drained her glass and refilled it.

'What if she's been hurt?' I asked, partly to distract her.

'Then she is hurt, or dead. How can we know? Or maybe she is taken by bad
guys, eh?' I thought she was actually beginning to enjoy it. 'Maybe she is
given bad time! Or maybe she escapes, yes? Who is of knowing?' She
plunked herself down in the chair again.

'You really don't give a damn, do you?'

'This is where you are wrong. She can do much damage to us if she is taken.
And if she is hurt, Nathalie will feel bad things.'

'What about you?'

She stood, and came to me and put a hand on my face and mocked me. 'You
poor boy! You think everyone must feel for everyone else like school friends!

This is big world little boy. Big world of big trouble.' She took her hand away. ' have of no luxury for caring.'

She just walked out.

Ten minutes later HH peered around the door and said in a voice that was too bloody cheerful 'Right old man. Nathalie and I are off.'

'But what about …' I began and the big man waved a dismissive hand.

'Nothing more to be done here.'

'What should I do?'

'To be honest old man, that's for you to decide. I'm sorry things haven't worked out for you and Sally the way you might have hoped. For now all we can do is make sure we keep our eyes and ears open and hope she's okay and gets in touch soon. If we hear anything, one of us will call.'

'I'm not sure if I'm staying.'

'Oh. Well, you might want to rethink that. Got to rush old man - take care.'

I followed him but by the time I reached the hall he and Nathalie were driving away. Alexandra was leaning against a wall, arms folded. I asked her if she was going with HH and Nathalie but she just shook her head slowly and wandered off.

Another day passed with no word of Sally. I didn't see Alexandra until the early evening when she came through the front doors with a gun in her hand looked at her as if to ask if there was trouble and she scowled and muttered 'Not yet' and disappeared again. It suddenly struck me she'd been left behind to baby-sit me and I didn't like it.

When it got too much and I'd drunk too much wine I went upstairs and packed a few things. I'd resolved to leave the next morning and to hell with them all. wasn't sure what I'd do, but I thought I'd start with London. I wrote a note for Sally ten times and still wasn't happy with it, but left it on the bed. I then wrote another note for Alexandra explaining where I was going and leaving an address and telephone number. I'd called an old wing man of mine and he was happy for me to stay with him for a few weeks until I got myself sorted.

I'd settled down and felt an unexpected huge relief at having made a decision If Sally returned and wanted to get in touch, that was up to her. Hopefully someone would let me know if they heard anything about or from her. I'd realised that staying around might prove pointless. If Sally returned there'd b exchanges between her and Alexandra and God knows Nathalie would have plenty to say about it. I had no idea how Sally would react and I'd stopped trying to guess.

hadn't fallen into a deep sleep so when I heard the noise outside I was up immediately. My watch told me it was three forty seven in the morning. There was the sound of a couple of vehicles and when I looked out of the French windows I could see headlights moving amongst the trees a few hundred yards away from the house. I knew there was no road through there and suspected bad things. Sally wouldn't have made such a show of returning.

Alexandra had given me a Browning automatic and a couple of clips and almost grinned as she watched me clumsily work the action. She demonstrated the proper way a few times and then threw the weapon at me and disappeared again. I grabbed it and crouched by the window. Above me I heard movement and crawled onto the balcony to look up. The silhouette against the moon was Alexandra's. I semi-whispered up at her and she hissed at me to get inside and keep down.

I stayed hunched up against the stone balustrades and peered into the gloom between the house and the trees. There were dark figures moving quickly and steadily towards the house. I counted five. They'd need to get a lot closer before I stood any chance of hitting anyone.

It was obvious that the opposition had either followed me or tracked Sally down somehow. It didn't really matter. It crossed my mind that maybe they'd got Sally and the thought made me start sweating.

I wouldn't have been that surprised if Nathalie and the two guys had suddenly appeared like the cavalry; but they didn't. What happened next did surprise me.

A single beam of light suddenly lit up the approaching figures and I heard a motorcycle engine roar. Then the shooting started. I heard Alexandra's rifle above me and another weapon out there in the darkness.

I gingerly raised my head to start shooting and then realised what was happening. A motorcycle was coming at the enemy sideways on and they were lit up in its headlight like rabbits. They were going down really quickly and most of the shooting was being done by the motorcycle rider. The bike went past the fallen bodies at a hell of a speed and disappeared. I couldn't make out the rider and was still watching it disappear when Alexandra dropped down onto the balcony.

I put it together pretty quickly and Alexandra just stood and watched as I did, rifle over her shoulder.

'What was ...' I began but stopped as Alexandra literally pushed me out of the way to come into the bedroom. She stormed off after snapping at me to stay put.

I followed the Russian but she was down and out of the house before I made the front door. There was nobody around and I couldn't hear anything moving.

I walked around the perimeter of the house not knowing what to expect. There was no sign of any vehicle. I made my way to d'Artagnan's paddock, half expecting to see the motorcycle abandoned and hear Sally chatting to the old horse. He just looked at me as if I was an unwelcome visitor and turned his back on me.

Of course there was no Sally. I made my way back to the house and light was coming up as I went in. Alexandra was sitting on the bottom of the stairs.

'Well?' I asked, not really expecting an answer.

'We wait. She decides. I ring Nathalie and others.'

'Does that mean you have done, or are going to?'

'Have.'

'Coming here?'

'Is no reason.' She got up and wandered towards the kitchen. Because I did know what else to do I followed her. She filled a kettle and put it on and then inspected the toaster before shoving a couple of slices of bread in. The rifle was on the huge wooden table as well as a Luger and a large knife.

'Are you going to tell me what happened?' I asked.

Alexandra busied herself with making toast and buttering it and began in a casual manner 'Opposition follow you. Sally saw them on way here. She follows. I am watching and see. She arrives and - poof! No more opposition

'For God's sake, I put that much together! But did you speak with her?'

Alexandra regarded me for a moment as if she was deciding whether to hit me or pity me. I think it was the latter because she said 'Yes. Few words. S has much to … she goes. Is for better.'

'Goes where? For how long?'

Alexandra shrugged and offered me toast.

'Please … just tell me.'

'She isn't knowing. I am sorry for you but … she has to be away. How long? She shrugged again. 'Is big guess.'

'Did she say anything about me?' I was desperate and must have sounded

No. Is nothing. You should eat.' She munched at the toast and I wandered off
o get myself ready to leave. By the time I'd got upstairs to the bedroom and
ooked out the window the bodies had been moved.

*   *   *   *   *

dropped the suitcase in the hall and put the note I'd written for Alexandra on
ne of the tables. The front doors were open and Alexandra was busying
erself in the engine compartment of a long wheel based Land Rover. She
jave me a cursory glance then fired the engine. She seemed happy with it
ind slammed the bonnet shut.

s from opposition' she said cheerily. 'They will not be needing. You need lift?'

said that it would be helpful. Alexandra strolled in and picked up my note.
She opened and read it, then folded it and put it in a pocket on her shirt. I said
d left a letter for Sally. As if this were some mystical cue, the old man
Maurice wandered up the steps. He looked serious and gingerly approached
ne. I looked into his watery blue eyes and they said more than he did about
vhat he handed me. It was an envelope and I recognised Sally's hand
mmediately.

lexandra tactfully wandered out with the old man and I went into the dining
oom to read Sally's letter.

My poor darling

orgive me but I can't face you. It would hurt us both too much.

*don't know how to explain. I've spent so much of my life with part of me
uried so deeply. I've had to. It's caught up with me a few times but never as
uch as with you. You really got me. I tried to shut you out, but it didn't work.
hat made me angry, and sad, and now I'm in bits. It's not your fault - it's me.*

*n not as strong as you think. You've seen me hurt, and do terrible things and
at is a part of me. But underneath all that, I'm not strong and that's why I
ave to hide myself away. I really think there's only room inside of me for one
ing, one dreadful thing, at least for the moment. I'm so sorry my love - and I
ally do love you - but I can't live a double life. I can't keep our love safe and
o what I have to.*

*ease try not to think too badly of me. I tried my best but it wasn't good
ough and I've let you down. I've let everyone down.*

ave to put myself back together and to do that I must go away.

*gain, please forgive me. I'm an impossible woman, I know that, and you're a
int for having put up with me for so long. Please find ways to be happy.*

x

*   *   *   *   *

Alexandra was sweet, or as close to it as I think she could get. She didn't question me and when I just blurted out whatever it was and shed tears she poured me drinks and sat with me. She told me not to reproach myself, that it was a difficult situation and that Sally was a complicated woman.

I didn't say a word to Alexandra as she drove me to the station. She wished me good luck and told me to look after myself.

Ten days after I arrived in London I got a telephone call. It was Nathalie and you could have knocked me down with a feather. She started off very formal and very official. She gave me a very blunt warning that I could never speak word about anything that I saw or heard, or what happened, under pain of serious injury or worse. I didn't ask her but she surprised me when she said

'She's all right by the way. Taking a break from it all, but she's all right.'

I thanked her for telling me. I thought she was probably worried I might try to find Sally in London so I reassured her I knew better.

'She's not here' Nathalie said sharply. 'She's a very long way away and I do know how long for.'

That worried me and I asked if it was work related.

'No; it's personal. About as personal as it gets. South America. There's a place she visits sometimes … family.'

I took this to mean Sally had returned to the place where she'd lost her parents and brother. I said I understood.

Nathalie changed the subject and asked if I had any plans. When I told her she said 'I've got something that might interest you. If you want a job, I know man who could use you. Security. Aircraft manufacturers. Managerial post.'

'I don't have any experience.'

'You can handle it.'

'Or references.'

'None needed. I spoke to him twenty minutes ago.'

I thanked her but got the impression she wanted me securely tucked away somewhere I wouldn't get up to any mischief.

don't know why - probably because Nathalie was as close to Sally as I
ealised anyone could be - but I asked her 'I didn't stand a chance, did I.'

'You did better than most.'

or a long time I questioned myself. Had I done all I could? Had Sally ever
een who I thought she was? And, worst of all, should I try to find her again?

ally Twitchett is larger than life. But she's also the most genuine girl I've ever
het. She has a heart, even 'though she keeps it buried much of the time, and
 driven by the need to fight for the right thing, to do some good. That's why
he won't stop working with Nathalie. God knows how many times they've
early lost their lives, but they won't stop.

he tragedy for Sally in her personal life is that she can't let anyone get close
 her. She fears for their safety too much and can't handle the distraction
ıch a relationship presents. But every so often she lets someone in, despite
 rself, and the latest was me.

ally is an impossible woman to love. But for me, it's impossible not to love
ər. She may be buried deep in my heart over time; but she won't ever go
vay.

EPILOGUE

year later I was pretty well set up. I'd called the bloke Nathalie had
commended me to and he couldn't have been nicer. He practically begged
e to take the job. I thought it would do as a start. I'd decided to give up
 eking adventure; I'd had enough of it for two lifetimes. The rest of the
 ɔkes in the job weren't up to much, which meant I got promoted pretty
 ιickly. I'm now Head of Security for a major aircraft corporation.

 ırt of my job is dealing with visiting VIPS - ministers and so forth. I make
 re nothing unpleasant comes their way.

 he day I was with a couple of my chaps and a very important man from the
 ates. He wanted to do some shopping in the King's Road, for his daughter
  said.

 we walked along the King's Road we passed a boutique called Fuzz. I
 ɔpped. My charge was impressed by the window display and insisted we go
  I could have sent my men in with him and gone back to the car to wait, but
 idn't.

 ɔleasant girl wearing a badge that said *"Call me Mavis"* came sliding up to
 offering help. While she engaged my American bloke, I looked around. In a
 ʰner at the back of the shop Nathalie Endeavour leaned against a wall. She
  s wearing a green silk mini dress and looked stunning and somehow

younger than I'd remembered her. She nodded curtly to me and I walked slowly to her.

Nathalie didn't wait for me to speak and said simply 'She's fine.'

'Back at it?'

'In a manner of speaking.'

'Where did she go?'

'I don't know. But she was back in two months.'

'Oh.' Had I hoped it would be longer? Did I want her to have gone through what I had for nearly a year? Of course not.

'You?'

Those huge round emerald eyes probed my soul as she raised her eyebrows and waited for an answer.

'The job worked out very well.'

'I know. I meant on a more personal level.'

'Pretty good. I'm actually thinking of getting engaged.'

'Good. Marriage will suit you.'

'We'll see. I'm glad she's OK.'

'Yes. Sally is OK.'

There were a few seconds of awkward silence and then I said I'd better get off. Nathalie said it was nice to see me and that she was glad things were working out well for me. She brushed past me and touched a hand to my shoulder and that was that.

I'm sure it was just an aberration brought on by memory but as I walked out of Nathalie's boutique I was sure I could smell Chanel Number 5.

I walked my American charge to the car, said goodbye and left the rest to my men. I wanted to walk, and remember.

It had been over a year since I'd last seen Sally Twitchett. As I started down the King's Road a white Mercedes Benz 230SL pulled out of the curb and into traffic just up the road. Maybe it was another coincidence misinterpreted because of memory but I was sure I saw a mass of golden hair in the driver's seat and above it a ridiculously long thin arm and hand waving as the Mercedes rocketed away.

urs later I found a small folded piece of paper in my pocket. It bore only a
ndon telephone number. I didn't have much doubt that Nathalie Endeavour
d put it there. It wasn't a Chelsea number so I knew it wasn't hers.

ank a lot of whisky and looked through the mail that had piled up on the
table. Amongst it were some travel brochures and one extolled the virtues
Brittany. The prospect of an engagement to be married seemed suddenly
y distant.

ed the telephone number but it just rang. I'd told myself I'd try it only once.
maybe one day …

Printed in Great Britain
by Amazon